成寒英語有聲書 ④

推理女神探

成　寒◎編著

K's First Case

目錄　K's First Case

K's First Case

如何使用本書

這部《推理女神探》是情境式的英語有聲書，一共有43
段，文體以結構簡單的句型，步步爲營，鋪陳出一個推理
故事，如歷現場。

1 先聽CD十遍，看你是否能聽出凶手是誰，使用何種凶
   器以及行凶手法，然後作聽力測驗。
2 學習方法：請參閱成寒著《英文，非學好不可》一
   書。

推理女神探

英語──現代的共同語言

張天鈞

　　在維也納美術史博物館有一張老彼得‧布勒哲爾（Pieter Bruegel the Elder, 1525-1569）畫的圖，十分特別，叫做巴別塔（The Tower of Babel），又稱通天塔，描繪一大堆工人在蓋一座巨塔，塔頂還被雲遮住，不過塔身正前方似乎塌陷了。其實這幅圖是在描繪聖經舊約創世紀第十一章的故事，那時天下人的口音、語言都是一樣的。他們在示拿地遇見一片平原，就商量說，我們要做磚，拿磚當石頭，又拿石漆當灰泥，要建造一座城和一座塔，塔頂通天，為要傳揚我們的名，免得我們分散在全地上。耶和華降臨要看世人所建的城和塔。

　　耶和華說，看哪，他們成為一樣的人民，都是一樣的言語，如今即做起這件事來，以後他們所要做的事，就沒有不成就的了。我們下去，在那裡變亂他們的口音，使他們的言語彼此不通。於是耶和華使他們從那裡分散在全地上。他們就停工不造那城了。因為耶和華在那裡變亂天下的言語，使眾人分散在全地上，所以那城名叫巴別，也就是變亂的意思。

　　現在到世界各地去開國際性會議，會議中規定使用的語言

巴別塔

通常是英文，而且重要的醫學期刊，也都規定用英文來撰寫論
文。其實早期的醫學以德國比較進步，因此我們在大學一年級
時（民國五十七年），還得修德文和拉丁文，而學拉丁文主要
是因為解剖學的名詞用拉丁文拼字的關係。

　　當然現在的醫學，以美國最為進步，並非美國人最聰明，
而是他們有好的研究環境，可以吸收來自世界各地極為優秀的
學生和科學家，自然而然的，英文就成為強勢的語言。但就法
國人而言，他們認為法語是最好聽的語言，所以在法國觀光
時，能講法語是比較受歡迎的，特別是他們一些藝術品的說
明，常常只用法語寫。

此外，大家使用共通的語言，對研究的溝通也十分有幫助。例如人類基因圖譜的解碼，就是靠許多國家的合作，才能將它完全定序。而台灣在這一方面，也扮演了一部分的角色。

現在我們可以經由網路搜尋某種疾病的最新進展，當然你可以點選所有的語言，也可以只點選英文，問題是，如果不是用英文撰寫論文，這樣別國的科學家可能看不懂，也就無法了解這篇研究的重要發現為何？

此外，由於科學的進步日新月異，每個人專精的，通常也只是一部分而已，所以彼此合作，才能夠成就偉大的發現，和完成較為複雜的研究，因此有共通的語言，在溝通上就容易多了，特別是在現在許多研究常常是跨國性的時候。

母語是美麗而又有豐富感情的，當然不能忘記，但為了知識的取得能與世界同步，英文的精通是十分必要的。怪不得許多英文補習班的廣告詞都寫著：不要讓小孩輸在起跑點。

可是談起學英語，許多人很容易會望之卻步，特別是要開口說英語時。記得以前曾在《讀者文摘》看過一篇文章，作者談到他如何容易的學會另一種語言，那就是不論在哪裡，在何時，例如一面吃飯或做其他事情的時候，一面聽錄音帶，很自然的就學會了那個語言。而且，語言是用來溝通的，用過分艱深的字眼，別人反而聽不懂，或造成誤會，因此重要的是如何把簡單的字用合乎文法的方式串連起來，寫成文章或講話。

【成寒英語有聲書】系列聽後給我的感覺，剛好就符合上述的想法。因為它可以在開車、散步、坐公車或捷運，甚至是做家事時，不知不覺的把英文學好，而且遇到外國人時，也可以字正腔圓，很自然的交談。學習英語變成快樂實用的一件事，也會充滿了成就感。而拜科技之賜，以CD有聲書出版，聽起來清晰又精采，也是現代人之福。

我們從小對語言的掌握和對事物的理解，都是在好奇心的驅使下，由東問西問開始，然後一步步增進了解。《成寒英語有聲書4──推理女神探》 這本有聲推理故事，以懸疑有趣的情節、生動的聲音語言，加上逼真的戲劇音效，充分誘導聽者（讀者）的好奇心，可以肯定是一優秀有益的英語課外讀本。

雖然在真實世界中，誰都上不了夢想中的巴別塔，然而聽故事，好聽的英語故事如【成寒英語有聲書】，卻能讓我們走遍世界自由行。

（本文作者爲臺大醫學院內科教授

暨臺大醫院代謝內分泌科主任）

▶ 前言

聽英語有聲書像福爾摩斯辦案子

成　寒

你以為我家裡會有很多書嗎？

老實跟你說，你看到架子上，留下來的，那些書幾乎全是未讀的。

你問，那麼已經讀過的呢？

告訴你好了，我這個人看書有隨看隨丟的習慣。書對我而言是「用過即丟」（disposable）而非「可收藏的」（collectable）。哎呀，你要罵我了，其實也不算丟啦，就是隨手給了別人。

從小到大，從彰化遷至台中—新竹—台北—美西—德國—美東，地球繞了一大圈，大搬家超過十回，如今暫在台北落腳，下一站說不定是上海或北京呢！你以為我會把一拖拉庫、三年之內都不想再看的舊書運來運去，付出高額的運費。別傻了，有些書到後來又想看，再買就是了。那麼，有些書難道不擔心它絕版？哦唷！絕版也就算了，個人又不在做什麼大學問，非得看什麼海內孤本不可。現在僱了個 part-time 助理，因為也愛看書，所以每個禮拜要她抱些書和雜誌回去。

丟書的速度比買還快，我家裡哪裡會有很多書。

書不以「冊」，而是以「捲」、「片」或「小時」計

不過，那也要看你對書的定義為何？有字的書隨看隨扔，可家裡的書還是不少，若論數量的話，恐怕也有上萬。

一直捨不得扔的是英語有聲書，德文有聲書也不少。《慾望城市》裡女專欄作家凱莉‧布雷蕭看到 Manolo Blahnik 牌的鞋子就想買，卻沒餘錢付頭期款買房子，差點沒地方住。我也是，一直以來都在租房子，但看到英語有聲書就有無法控制的購買慾。

那要有多大的房子才放得下上萬「冊」有聲書？

我的有聲書不是以「冊」，而是以「捲」或「片」計。以前錄音帶時代，可能需要有棟大房子才裝得下，而今情況大不同。我書櫃裡有一整套一千三百多部名著改編的英語廣播劇，全部收錄在二十片MP3裡，量一下高度，不過像一冊大部頭《卡拉馬助夫兄弟們》精裝版那般厚。

二○○三年暑假我到南部辦簽名會，有個年約三十歲的男讀者走過來，秀出他腰間皮帶上搭扣著一具小小的玩意兒，我原以為是手機，但實際上是厚如手機，面積卻更小。一問，原來是錄音筆，他把七個小時的有聲書全裝在裡頭，而小小圓頭耳機就塞在耳朵裡。他說成天忙亂，沒時間好好坐下專心聽，只有走路的時候才有空聽英文。算一算，每天走來走去走掉不少時間，半年下來，倒也聽了不少英語有聲書。試想，七個小

時的有聲書，足夠放進整本福爾摩斯探案《四簽名》或《大亨小傳》或海明威《流動的饗宴》，綽綽有餘。

伊什梅爾跳到面前來

「叫我伊什梅爾。」（Call me Ishmael.）堪稱美國文學最知名的開場白。看文字，感覺或許不深；但聽英語有聲書朗讀，這個旁白人物陡然鮮明起來，跳到面前，帶出美國文學中最神祕的角色──大白鯨，這部關於探索未知的巨作，關於理性與邪惡的交戰，也是充滿隱喻與象徵的小說。當捕鯨船上的人全數犧牲，只剩下伊什梅爾一人活在世上藉由梅爾維爾的筆說故事。我的《白鯨記》有二十七個鐘頭。

初聽一部英語有聲書的過程，有如福爾摩斯在辦案子，使用「演繹法」（deduction）：「當你一一消除掉所有的不可能，剩下的那個，不管是多麼不可能，一定就是你要的答案！」（When you have eliminated the impossible, whatever remains, however improbable, must be the truth.）──《四簽名》（The Sign of Four），但方法剛好相反：「當你聽出一個又一個可能的關鍵字，剩下的那個，不管是多麼不可能，經過反覆練習，最後還是可能給你聽了出來！」

比方說懸疑廣播劇，第一次先聽出個大概，知道主角是誰、背景在哪兒、約略發生了什麼事，以及犯案手法，然後每多聽一次宛若一層層抽絲剝繭，剝出被害人、加害人、犯案動機，背後的疑點，一條條線索漸次浮現，細節越來越清晰。

假使在過程當中有點分心，一閃神，漏掉了一兩個重要關鍵字，就像錯過一個重要的線索，這個案子就無法偵破了。

這期間，你當然要另外多聽一些別的，多背一些單字和片語，觸類旁通──從此案延伸推測彼案。到最後，有聲書可能已經聽了幾十遍，還沒真正看過一眼書的內文，然而本來不認識的一些單字經過耳朵多次過濾，洗淨，腦波轉換，動盪推敲，哇！後來竟然給你聽了出來，整齣戲頓時現出全貌──這個案子，原來如此啊！

想到《遠離非洲》（*Out of Africa*）作者伊莎克‧丹妮蓀（Isak Dinesen），她年輕時喜歡在情人的面前說書給他聽，伴著留聲機低低吟唱。所以她寫的書都像在你面前說故事，十分動人。倘若當時有人幫她錄下，想必又是一部部精采好聽的有聲書。

大家都知道，海明威的文風是非常簡潔的，每個句子都是短短的。有一次，我聽到一段話："He was dead and that was all."（他死了，一切都結了。）只有海明威才寫得出這句話。聽人朗讀，彷彿能感受到那個人已經斷了氣，到句點戛然而止。

英文如數學，句型像公式

我唸國中的時候，導師是國文老師，她很喜歡我，因為我總是代表學校出去參加作文比賽，而且我也很用功，其他功課都很好，就是英文數學怎麼讀也讀不好。

老師很同情又很疼惜地對我說：「數學不好可能是天生的，這可以理解，但就是不明白為什麼妳的英文也不好。國文較佳的人英文通常也會比較好。」

這個問題直到今天我才豁然明白：原來當年的英文教學法是把英文當成數學，一字字、一句句分析講解，一題題文法句型就好像套用數學公式，像我這種沒數學腦筋的，怪不得怎麼學也學不好。

語言，不就是「模仿」及「重複」嗎？

語言的敏感度要靠長期大量的「閱讀」和大量的「聽」來培養，文法有其必要，但只是入門的捷徑。有一次，作家蔡素芬應雜誌之邀，寫一篇關於女畫家歐姬芙（Georgia O'Keeffe）的文章，提到她的畫尤其是放大的花具有「性象徵」（sex symbol），編輯看稿時擅自更改為「象徵性」。你說這兩個一模一樣的詞，僅掉換次序，有何不同？若按我從前的英文老師作法，也許可以用文法分析解釋一堆，但我們只要憑「感覺」就知道哪個字的用法才是對的。

*   *   *

另一例子，最近我看到一篇獲文學獎的短篇小說，其中提到「有羅麗塔情節的男子」，乍讀之下，你知道這句話有錯嗎？

——「羅麗塔情節」指發生中年男子愛上「幼齒」的一段故事情節。

──「羅麗塔情結」指這個男子有戀「幼齒」的偏好。

「羅麗塔」這個字出自俄裔美籍作家納博可夫（Vladimir Nabokov, 1899-1977）的文學經典《羅麗塔》（*Lolita*），敘述一名中年男子愛上小女孩羅麗塔，故意娶了女孩的母親。然而在無意間，小女孩的母親發現此事，一氣之下衝出家門，不幸被車子撞死，男子於是帶著羅麗塔開車遊遍美國。書出版後備受爭議，榮登一九五九年紐約時報暢銷書排行榜。在一九六二和一九九七年兩度改編成電影。

「羅麗塔」（Lolita）已成為精神病學上中年男子戀上未成年少女或「戀童癖」（pedophilia）的代名詞。

另一類似的詞彙是「五月與十二月」（May-December）：愛上年齡差距極大的異性。

＊　　　　＊　　　　＊

形容人的皮膚很「白」，英文習慣用 "fair" 而不是 "white"；例句：「她是金髮白膚。」（She has blond hair and fair skin.），除非是配合其他字變成形容詞「像牛奶般白的皮膚」（milky white skin）。電影《一樹梨花壓海棠》（*Lolita*），男主角形容小妖精羅麗塔的皮膚很白，也是用 "fair" 這個字，但中文字幕卻譯成「皮膚很好」──皮膚白並不一定是皮膚好。

某晚聽了一齣福爾摩斯探案廣播劇〈法蘭西絲・卡法克斯女士的失蹤〉（The Disappearance of Lady Frances Carfax），

女僕形容帶走女主人的那個傢伙是「黑的」（black）。華生醫生納悶地反問，黑人？可妳不是說他是英國人？女僕說他是啊，但曬得很黑。華生醫生恍然大悟，哦！原來是 "tan"。瞧，些微之差，只憑感覺。

＊　　　　＊　　　　＊

推理女神探的原作者

　　《推理女神探》這篇故事的作者 ──路易·亞歷山大（Louis Alexander）一九三二年生於倫敦，一九五四年畢業於倫敦大學。他是著名的英語語言教學專家，對英語學習有著獨到的見解和豐富的經驗，曾在好幾個國家教過英文。他的作品包括《新觀念英語》（*New Concept English*，1967，大陸版《新概念英語》）等。

　　《推理女神探》在許多歐洲國家列為國中生必讀英語課外讀物，尤其是在德國，十三、四歲的少年都對這個故事耳熟能詳，不僅練習英語聽力，同時也學到推理分析能力。

＊有關英文學習的問題，**請參閱成寒著《英文，非學好不可》一書。**

推理女神探

有聲書內文

The Victim
被害人

CD＊1

The people in the story:

This is a murder story.

This man was the victim.
His name was Michael Gray.
He was fifty-five years old. He was very rich.
He was a Director of Selkirk Industries.

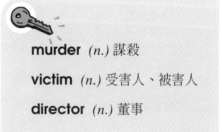

murder *(n.)* 謀殺

victim *(n.)* 受害人、被害人

director *(n.)* 董事

The Woman Detective

女警探

CD ＊2

Look at this woman.
She is young and pretty, and she is very clever.
She is a detective.
Her name is Kathy Kirby.
People call her "K".
She wants to find the answers to some important questions.
This is her first case.
Can you help her?

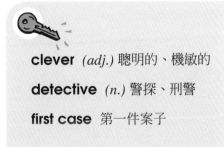

clever *(adj.)* 聰明的、機敏的

detective *(n.)* 警探、刑警

first case 第一件案子

K, our clever detective, has three important questions:

X murdered the victim, Michael Gray, so

1. How did X murder Mr. Gray?

2. Who was X?

3. Why did X murder Mr. Gray?

HOW...? WHO...? WHY...?

important *(adj.)* 重要的

X *(n.)* 大寫或小寫字母，代表未知數，此處是指凶手。

Who was X?

誰是 X ？

C D ＊3

How...? Who...? Why...?

Who was X?

There was a murder. There were five other people in the house at the time. One of them was X. Who was it ?

Elizabeth Gray,
Michael Gray's wife.
She is forty-eight years old.

Colonel William Stevens,
Mr. Gray's friend.
He is fifty years old.
He was in the army years ago, but he isn't in the army now.

Miss Angela Everett,
Mr. Gray's secretary.
She has been Mr. Gray's
secretary for a year.
She is twenty-five years old.

Mr. Andrew Selkirk,
Mrs. Gray's brother.
He is forty years old.
He is a Director of
Selkirk Industries, too.

Mrs. Nancy Baker,
She is the Grays' housekeeper.
She has been with Mrs. Gray's
family for forty years.
She is sixty years old.

at the time 在事情發生的時候

colonel *(n.)* 上校

in the army 在軍中服務

secretary *(n.)* 祕書

the Grays 葛瑞家（如張家、李家、王家）

housekeeper *(n.)* 女管家

What happened?

發生了什麼事？

C D ＊4

What happened?

The date：November 17th, 1982

The time now: 10:15

The place：A large country house in New England.

Mr. Gray had dinner with four of the other people at eight o'clock this evening. Then he went to his study. The time was nine o'clock. He locked the door from the inside. He closed the window, too, and locked it from the inside.

At 9:30, the housekeeper, Mrs. Baker, took some coffee to his room. She knocked on the door. Mr. Gray didn't answer, so she knocked again and shouted. He didn't answer, so she called three of the other people. They knocked on the door, too, and shouted, but Mr.

Gray didn't open it. They broke down the study door and went in. They saw Mr. Gray's body on the floor. Mr. Gray was dead.

Mrs. Gray called the police. The time was 9:40. The police arrived at 9:50, and K arrived with them.

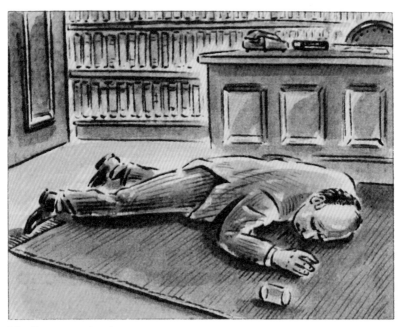

Mr. Gray was dead.

country house （貴族、富豪等的）鄉間大宅邸

New England 新英格蘭區：指美國東北部地區，包括康乃狄克州(Connecticut)、麻州(Massachusetts)、羅德島(Rhode Island)、佛蒙特州(Vermont)、新罕布夏州(New Hampshire)、緬因州(Maine)等六個州。

study *(n.)* 書房

lock *(v.)* 鎖上、鎖住

inside *(n.)* 內部、裡面

knock *(v.)* 敲（門）

break down 破壞、毀壞（break的過去式及過去分詞: broke, broken）

on the floor 在地板上

arrive *(v.)* 抵達

What the police found?

警方查到了什麼？

ＣＤ＊5

Now it's 10:15, and K is in the study.

Mr. Gray's dead body isn't here now. The police took photographs of the study and photographs of the body. Then they took the body to the police station. A police doctor has already looked at the body. The police already know the answer to three important questions.

1. Mr. Gray didn't die of poison. He drank some whisky at 9:20, but there wasn't any poison in the whisky and there wasn't any poison in Mr. Gray's blood.

2. X stabbed Mr. Gray through the heart with a sharp weapon.

3. Mr. Gray died at 9:25.

A policeman called K from the police station. "We know three things," the policeman said. "The first thing is: it wasn't poison. The second thing is: it was a sharp weapon–through the heart. The third thing is: Mr. Gray died at 9:25."

"We know three things," the policeman said.

police station 警察局

police doctor 法醫

die of poison 死於中毒

whisky *(n.)* 威士忌酒

stab *(v.)* 刺、戳

through *(prep.)* 穿過、穿透

sharp weapon 尖銳的凶器

Mr. Gray's house

葛瑞先生的房子

CD＊6

The house:

Look at this photograph of Mr. Gray's house. Its name is 'Longacres'. It's a very big house. There are eight bedrooms upstairs. Downstairs there's a hall and a kitchen and there are four big rooms–a dining room, a living room, a study and a library.

'Longacres'

Here is a plan of the rooms downstairs. Look at the plan carefully. Mr. Gray had dinner with the four other people at eight o'clock this evening. That was in the dining room. Then he went to his study at nine o'clock.

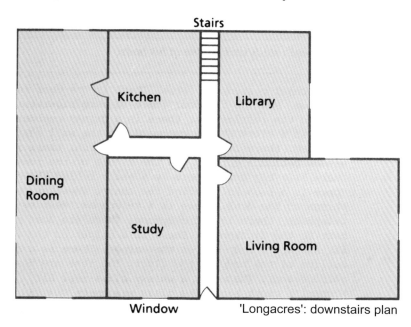

Stairs

Kitchen   Library

Dining Room

Study

Living Room

Window   'Longacres': downstairs plan

bedroom *(n.)* 臥室

upstairs *(adv.)* 樓上

downstairs *(adv.)* 樓下

hall *(n.)* 門廊、門廳

dining room 餐廳

living room 客廳

library *(n.)* 藏書室

plan *(n.)* 平面圖

The study and the murder

書房與謀殺

CD＊7

The study and the murder:

The murder happened in Mr. Gray's study. Here is a police photograph of the study. Look at it carefully and describe it. Then read K's report.

Mr. Gray's study and outline of his body.

(K's report:)

Mr. Gray's study is large. There is one door into the room. Next to the door there is a refrigerator. Next to the refrigerator there is a liquor cabinet. There is a clock on the cabinet. On the wall near the cabinet there is a picture. On the right there is a window behind the curtain. In the middle of the room there is a big desk. There is a chair behind the desk. There is a bookcase behind the chair. There are some things on the desk. There is a telephone. Next to the telephone there is a dictaphone. There are some papers next to the dictaphone. There is a carpet on the floor.

Mr. Gray's body was on the carpet. There is a police outline of the body on the floor. The feet are near the refrigerator. There was a whisky glass near Mr. Gray's right hand. The glass was empty.

carefully *(adv.)* 仔細地、小心地

describe *(v.)* 形容、描述

report *(n.)* 報告

next to 在…的旁邊

refrigerator *(n.)* 冰箱（口語: fridge）

liquor *(n.)* 烈酒、含酒精的飲料

liquor cabinet *(n.)* 酒櫃

curtain *(n.)* 窗簾

bookcase *(n.)* 書櫃

dictaphone *(n.)* 口述錄音機

carpet *(n.)* 地毯

outline *(n.)* 輪廓、輪廓圖

The clues

線 索

C D ✳8

The clues:

Now look at the clues carefully and describe them. Then read K's report.

K found these things:

Empty whisky glass on the floor next to Mr. Gray's right hand. Drop of whisky and water in glass.

Blood and water on Mr. Gray's shirt. A hole in the shirt. X stabbed Mr. Gray through the heart.

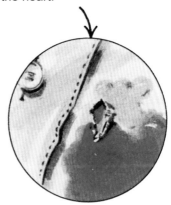

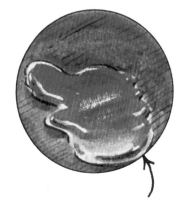

Blood and water
on the carpet.

Door locked from
the inside.

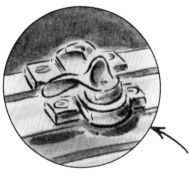

Window locked
from the inside.

K didn't find these things:

Other fingerprints:
only Mr. Gray's.

There weren't any weapons.
There wasn't a knife or gun.

There aren't any
secret doors or
passages.

The locked room

鎖上的房間

CD＊9

(K's report:)

Mr. Gray's body was in front of the refrigerator. His feet were near the refrigerator. He was on the carpet face down.

The whisky glass was empty. I smelled it. It was in Mr. Gray's right hand at the time of the murder. There was blood and water on Mr. Gray's shirt–over his heart. X stabbed Mr. Gray with a sharp weapon. There was blood and water on the carpet. X stabbed Mr. Gray with a sharp weapon, so there was blood on Mr. Gray's shirt and there was blood on the carpet. But why was there water on Mr. Gray's shirt and water on the carpet?

Mr. Gray locked the door from the inside and the window from the inside. There were fingerprints on the desk, on the refrigerator and on the whisky glass, but they were only Mr. Gray's fingerprints. There aren't any secret passages in the room. There wasn't a knife or a gun in the room. Mr. Gray's dictaphone was on.

K is writing notes for her report.

in front of 在…之前

face down 趴著

smell *(v.)* 聞、嗅

shirt *(n.)* 襯衫

fingerprint *(n.)* 指紋

secret passage 祕密通道

knife *(n.)* 刀

K's first theory

K的第一個理論

CD＊10

Is this what happened?
K's first theory:

9:00　Mr. Gray came into the study and locked the door from the inside.

9:02　He closed the window and locked it from the inside.

9:05　He sat at his desk and wrote. Then he used the dictaphone.

9:20 He went to the liquor cabinet. He poured a glass of whisky and drank some.

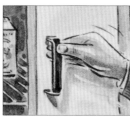

9:22 He went to the refrigerator. He wanted some ice.

9:25 X came into the room and stabbed Mr. Gray with a sharp weapon. Then X left.

9:30 Mrs. Baker knocked on the door and called three of the other people.

9:35 They broke down the door.

 9:40　Mrs. Gray called the police.

 9:50　The police and K arrived.

Is this theory right? Then how did X get into the room, and how did he or she get out? The window and door were locked from the inside. There aren't any secret doors or passages. Why is there water on Mr. Gray's shirt and on the floor?

theory *(n.)* 理論

Other theories
其他的理論

CD＊11

Other theories:

K's first theory is not very good. Think of other theories. Then compare them with K's.

K's second theory

It was suicide. No. Why? Because there wasn't any poison in the whisky and there wasn't any poison in Mr. Gray's blood. Did Mr. Gray use a knife? No. Why? Because there isn't a knife in the room. So it wasn't suicide.

think of 想想看、想到

compare...with 與…相比、與…做一比較

suicide *(n.)* 自殺

K's third theory

X was already in the room. He or she murdered Mr. Gray with a knife and left. X took the knife (or sharp weapon) with him (or her). No. Why? The door was locked from the inside, and the window was locked from the inside.

K's fourth theory

X used the keyhole. No. Why? The key was in the lock.

Did you think of other theories?
Did you compare them with K's?
How did they compare?

leave *(v.)* 離開、離去（過去式及過去分詞：left）

X took the knife with him. X把刀帶走了。

keyhole *(n.)* 鑰匙孔

Michael Gray's habits

麥可‧葛瑞的習慣

ＣＤ＊12

Michael Gray's habits
K's report:

Mr. Gray arrived
home at 7:00 this
evening. He arrived
with his secretary,
Angela Everett.
Mr. Gray *always*
arrives home at
this time, but his
secretary doesn't
always come with
him.

Colonel Stevens and Andrew Selkirk were already at 'Longacres'. They arrived at 5:00 in the afternoon. They had a drink with Mrs. Gray. Mrs. Baker served drinks in the library.

At 7:00 Mr. Gray went to his room. He took a bath and changed for dinner. He *always* takes a bath and changes at this time. Then he went to the library and had a drink with his wife, Colonel Stevens, Andrew Selkirk and Angela Everett. Mr. Gray *always* has a drink before dinner.

Dinner was at 8:00.
Mr. Gray *always*
has dinner at 8:00.
They all had dinner
in the dining room.
They all sat around
the table and talked.

drink *(n.)* 酒、飲料

have a drink 喝一杯（過去式：had a drink）

serve drinks 端來酒、送來飲料

take a bath 沐浴（過去式：took a bath）

change *(v.)* 更衣

Mrs. Baker answers some questions

貝克太太答問

CD＊13

Mrs. Baker answers some questions:

K sat in Mr. Gray's chair in the study and spoke to Mrs. Baker.

"So they all had dinner and talked, Mrs. Baker?" K asked.

"Yes, ma'am," Mrs. Baker said.

"Did they laugh too, Mrs. Baker?"

"Oh, yes, ma'am. They're all good friends."

"Good friends, Mrs. Baker?"

"Yes–well, er–Mr. Gray and Mrs. Gray, well– they..."

"They argued, Mrs. Baker? "

"Yes, ma'am, but not at dinner. After dinner Mr. Gray and Mrs. Gray went to the library. Just the two of them. They argued. I heard them. I was in the kitchen. They shouted and shouted. We all heard them."

"Then what?"

Mrs. Baker answers some questions.

"Then Mr. Gray went to his study."

"What time was that?"

"It was nine o'clock."

ma'am *(n.)* 女士、夫人、小姐(對女性的尊稱；＝madam)

argue *(v.)* 爭執、爭吵

Just the two of them. 只有他們兩人。

More questions

繼續追問

CD＊14

"Did Mr. Gray always go to his study at nine o'clock?"

"Yes, ma'am. He worked in his study until 1:00 or 2:00 in the morning. Sometimes his secretary went to his study with him," Mrs. Baker said.

"Sometimes? Did she go there this evening?"

"No, ma'am. I took Mr. Gray a cup of coffee at 9:30. I always take him a cup of coffee at 9:30. I knocked on the study door, but he didn't answer. I knocked again and again. I shouted, but he didn't answer, so I called Mrs. Gray, Colonel Stevens, and Mr. Selkirk."

"And Miss Everett?"

"No, ma'am. She was in the garden. Colonel Stevens and Mr. Selkirk broke down the door, and we found him–Mr. Gray–we found him on the floor–dead! Oh!" Mrs. Baker cried. She was very sad.

"Thank you, Mrs. Baker," K said quietly.

We found him on the floor.

 again and again 一次又一次

quietly (*adv.*) 平靜地、（聲音）輕柔地

Elizabeth Gray's story

伊麗莎白・葛瑞的說辭

CD ＊15

Elizabeth Gray's story:

Mrs. Baker left the study, and K wrote her report. Then there was a knock on the door. It was very quiet.

"Come in," K said quietly.

The door opened.

"You wanted to see me," Mrs. Gray said.

"Yes, Mrs. Gray. Come in and sit down please. A drink?"

"No, thank you."

"How are you?" K asked quietly.

"How can you ask? Mike's gone. He's dead. Dead! It isn't true, is it, Detective Kirby? It isn't true."

"Sh!" K said. "Tell me about him."

"You wanted to see me."
Elizabeth Gray said.

"Mike? He was a good husband. We got married twenty-five years ago. That's a long time, isn't it? He was just out of the army then. He loved me and I loved him. We didn't have any children, and Mike was always sorry about that. But he was always a good husband to me."

"Always?"

"Yes, always!" Mrs. Gray shouted. "Well–there were..."

"Yes?" K asked quietly.

"Other women. All these secretaries!" Mrs. Gray cried. "Mike always liked young secretaries–and they liked him. For his money! Look at this new one. This... this...What's her name? This Angela Everett. The little...! " Mrs. Gray's voice was quiet, but her face was red and her eyes were angry.

"Oh," she said, "I hated Mike's secretaries. They were always young, always pretty, and they took him away from me. But I really hate this secretary. This Angela Everett. She comes into my house every day. She comes with Mike. 'I'm sorry, Mrs. Gray,' she says in her pretty little voice. 'I have to take Mr. Gray from you. We have work to do.' Mike loved me. I know it! I know it! But he liked other women. He was rich, so women liked him. Yes. I loved Mike, but

"I loved him and I hated him."

sometimes, I hated him. I hated him! Maybe he's in this room now. Maybe he can hear me. I loved him and I hated him. He knew that well."

"What happened this evening?" K asked.

"I'll tell you," Mrs. Gray said.

quiet *(adj.)* 安靜的、輕聲的

out of the army 離開軍中、退伍

After dinner 晚餐後   C D＊16

Can I speak to you, Mike – in the library?

Yes, Liz.

What is it, Liz?

It's about... this... this secretary.

Angela? Yes.

She's a wicked woman, Mike. I know it. She wants your money.

That's not true, Liz.

It is! I know it.

She's a good secretary, Liz. I can't work without a secretary.

I don't like her, Mike. She's wicked.

Well, I like her and she's my secretary.

Please, Mike, I don't want to fight.

I'm not fighting. You are.

Please listen, Mike.

I won't listen. It's always the same with you. You're jealous.

You're jealous.

I'm not... and don't shout.

I'm not shouting.

I'm going to my study. I have work to do.

Please, Mike. Listen... I'm sorry.

＊Liz 為Elizabeth的小名
＊Mike 為Michael的小名

Called the police

叫警察

CD＊17

"So Mr. Gray went to his study at nine o'clock. What did you do?" K asked.

"I went to the living room. I wanted to speak to my brother, Andrew. We sat and talked. I told him about Mike and about that woman, Everett. Andrew knows all about it."

"Can I go now?" Mrs. Gray asked suddenly.

"Mr. Gray was in the study. Did you hear him?"

"No. At 9:30 Nancy shouted. Andrew and I ran to the study. The door was locked. Andrew and Colonel Stevens broke down the door. Then I saw Mike's body on the floor. He was dead! I called the police."

"Where was Miss Everett?" K asked.

"In the garden. She often went to the study after dinner."

"But not tonight?"

"No. Not tonight. She was in the garden. Why did Mike die? It wasn't suicide, so maybe she knows. Maybe she can tell you. A woman like that cannot bring good to this house. Can I go now?" Mrs. Gray asked suddenly.

"Of course," K said. "Thank you, Mrs. Gray."

good *(n.)* 好處、利益、幸福

cannot bring good to this house 對這個家沒有好處

Colonel Stevens's story

史蒂文斯上校的說辭

ＣＤ＊18

Colonel Stevens's story:

The time was 10:45. There was a knock on the study door.

"Can I come in?" a voice asked. It was a man's voice.

"Yes," K said.

The door opened and Colonel Stevens came in. "You want to see all of us tonight. Detective Kirby?"

"Yes," K said. "A drink, Colonel Stevens?"

"Yes, please."

"Whisky?"

"Yes, please. I need one!"

"Ice?"

"Ice? Er–er–no, thank you. I don't want any ice. Just water, please. Thank you."

"He was your friend?" K asked.

"Yes. A very good friend, too," the Colonel said. He put his head between his hands. "Dead! Michael

"Dead! Michael Gray dead! I can't believe it."

Gray dead! I can't believe it."

"It's sad," K said, "but it's true."

"Tell me about him," K said.

"We were in the army together. That was twenty-five years ago. Then Michael left the army, married Elizabeth and went into Selkirk Industries. That's Mrs. Gray's family firm. She was a Selkirk. I left the army five years ago. I'm not in the army now but people call me 'Colonel'. I needed work so I went to my old friend, Michael. He helped me."

"Helped you? How?" K asked.

"Oh–er–um. Money. You know."

"I don't know," K said.

"He gave me money."

"*Gave* you?"

"Lent me."

"How much did he lend you?"

"$100,000."

"Mm. And what did you do with it?"

"I put it into my business."

"What *is* your business, Colonel Stevens?"

"Well, it isn't really a *business*...horses...you know."

"You gambled the money," K said sharply.

"Yes, I gambled and lost," the Colonel said. "Michael knew about this. He was very angry with me. He said, 'I lent you this money, and now you have to pay it back to me.' I said, 'I can't. I don't have any money!' He said, 'Then you have to sell your house!' I didn't want to sell my house. We argued about this."

"He's dead now," K said. "Are you *really* sorry?"

"Sorry? Of course I'm sorry. We argued about money, but we were friends. Good friends. Army friends are always good friends."

"What did you do in the army, Colonel?"

"I was with the engineers. Michael was with the engineers, too."

"Are you an engineer?"

"I *was* an engineer."

"And now you gamble with other people's money," K said sharply.

"I gambled and lost."

"You argued with Mr. Gray about money. Tell me about it."

family firm 家族企業

She was a Selkirk. 她是謝爾柯克家的人。如同電影明星阿諾的老婆 Maria Shriver, "She is a Kennedy." 意思是「她是甘迺迪家的人」。

lend *(v.)* 借貸、出借（過去式及過去分詞：lent ）

gamble *(v.)* 賭博

sharply *(adv.)* 尖銳地、銳聲地

lose *(v.)* 失掉、輸掉（過去式及過去分詞：lost）

angry with 對…很生氣

pay back 償還

engineer *(n.)* 工程師、工兵

the engineers 工兵部隊

Gambled and lost 賭輸了錢 CD＊19

A pretty little thing
漂亮的小姑娘

C D ＊20

"Tell me about tonight."

"Tonight? After dinner I went to the living room. I went with Andrew. Michael and Elizabeth went to the library. They argued. We heard them from the living room. They often argued, Michael and Elizabeth. Michael–you know–he liked women. And Angela, well, she's a pretty little thing." The Colonel smiled. "Like you, Detective Kirby. A pretty little thing."

"Like you, Detective Kirby. A pretty little thing."

"Thank you, Colonel," K smiled. "What did you do after dinner?"

"Well, Michael went to his study. Elizabeth came to the living room, and I went to the library. I sat in the library and read."

"Alone?"

"Yes, alone. The housekeeper, Mrs. Baker, brought me some coffee at 9:30. Then she took some coffee to Michael. His door was locked. She shouted. I ran to the study. You know the story."

"Yes, but not all the story–yet!" K said sharply. "You can go now, Colonel, and please call Miss Everett for me."

alone *(adj.)* 單獨的、獨自一人

Angela Everett's story
安琪拉・艾佛瑞的說辭

CD＊21

Angela Everett's story:

"I don't like this room," Miss Everett said. "Mick died in here. Only two hours ago–Mick died in here. Why do you use this room?"

"I have my reasons," K said. "Sit down. Miss Everett. A drink?"

"Yes, please. A very large whisky and a lot of ice, please."

K went to the refrigerator. She opened it, then she opened the freezer and took out the ice-tray. She put some ice in Miss Everett's drink and then put the ice-tray back in the freezer. K looked into the freezer, then she looked at Miss Everett.

"Why are you looking at me?" Miss Everett asked suddenly.

"Colonel Stevens calls you 'a pretty little thing'. *Are* you?" K asked sharply.

"Are *you*?" Miss Everett asked. She spoke sharply too.

"I'm asking the questions," K answered. "Here's your drink."

"Thanks."

"He loved you."

"Of course he did. Didn't *she* tell you?"

"*She*?"

"That woman. His wife. *She* didn't love him. *She* fought with him. All the time. *She* fought with my Mick."

"Colonel Stevens calls you 'a pretty little thing'."

"Mick?"

"Yes, he was 'Mick' to me. 'Mike' to *her*. 'Michael' to other people. My Mick loved me. *She* always shouted at him, fought with him. So he always came to me. *She* gave him hate. I gave him love."

"You really loved him?"

"Of course. I loved him deeply. And *she* knew it. I hate her. I hate that woman," Miss Everett shouted. "*She* hated my Mick and *I* hate *her*. She murdered him. I know it. I know it."

"Mr. Gray was fifty-five. And you are twenty-five."

"What are you saying?" Miss Everett asked sharply. "Don't you know any nice men of fifty-five? Mick was nice. Really nice."

"And rich," K said sharply. "He left a lot of money to you, in his will."

"Really? How do you know that?"

"I'm asking the questions, and you are answering them," K said. "You knew about the money."

"And rich," K said sharply.

"Yes," Miss Everett answered.

"How much did he leave you?"

"I don't know."

"You know very well. Tell me," K said sharply.

"Mick changed his will two weeks ago. He left a lot of money to *her*, of course. *She* doesn't need money. *She's* rich. But he left $200,000 to me. He told me about it."

"Mr. Gray is dead now, and that's a good thing for you."

"Good for me? What are you saying? I loved him. Don't you understand?"

"Yes, but maybe you're rich now. Maybe you have $200,000."

"Jealous?" Miss Everett asked K sharply. "Listen, policewoman, I love money. That's true. But I loved Mick. Do you hear? I loved Mick. Why did the police send a woman detective?"

"Ask them," K said.

"You're pretty," Miss Everett said. "My Mick liked pretty women. His wife was a pretty woman years ago, but she isn't now."

"I must tell her that," K said.

"Yes. Tell her. Please tell her!"

"You often went to the study with Mr. Gray after

"Listen, policewoman, I love money."

dinner."

"Yes. We worked together. We usually went to the study at 9:00. I usually had a drink with Mick. Then we worked. The housekeeper usually brought us a cup of coffee at 9:30. I worked till 11:00, then I went home."

"But you didn't go to Mr. Gray's study tonight?"

"No, I didn't. It's strange."

"Strange?"

"Yes, Mick didn't want me to go. He wanted to be alone."

"Tell me about it."

註：這段情節提到K放了一些冰塊（some ice）在艾佛瑞小姐的威士忌酒裡，但在ＣＤ＊２７，K卻又說只給了艾佛瑞小姐一塊冰塊，顯然作者有些矛盾。

"He wanted to be alone."

freezer *(n.)* 冰箱的冷凍庫

ice-tray *(n.)* 製冰格

fight *(v.)* 爭吵、爭執（過去式及過去分詞：fought）

will *(n.)* 遺囑

jealous *(adj.)* 嫉妒的

In the car on the way home 回家途中

CD＊22

Will we work tonight, Mick?

Work? No, Angela.

I want to work alone tonight.

Mick...

Yes?

Will you work on your will?

Maybe.

My little Mick loves his little Angela.

Of course.

Little Mick won't change his will again?

I don't want to talk about my will.

My Mick loves his Angela and doesn't love that woman!

Angela! I've told you before. Don't speak about Elizabeth like that!

Mick! Careful!

SCREEECH

Angela! Sometimes I get very angry with you!

Changed the will
修改遺囑

CD＊23

"And where were you tonight–at the time of the murder?"

"In the garden."

"Where, in the garden?"

"Outside Mick's study."

"Why?"

"I wanted to walk. It was a cold night, but it was clear. I needed air. Mick was in his study. I wanted to be with him, and I was alone. I didn't want to stay in the house."

"You were afraid," K said.

"Afraid? Why?"

"Maybe Mr. Gray wanted to change his will again. You were afraid of that. You didn't want that, did you?"

"That's not true. I only wanted to be with him. It wasn't the money."

"You want to be a rich woman."

"Quiet!" Miss Everett shouted. "I'm pretty and you hate me. You like *her*. Well, listen. I didn't do it. See? I didn't do it!" Miss Everett shouted. Then she ran out of the room.

Then she ran out of the room.

clear *(adj.)* 晴朗的

afraid *(adj.)* 害怕的、恐懼的、擔心的

Andrew Selkirk's story
安德魯‧謝爾柯克的說辭

CD＊24

Andrew Selkirk's story:

"Can I come in?" a voice said. The voice was cool, aristocratic.

"Yes, and shut the door, please," K said. She looked up.

"It's me. Andrew Selkirk. Miss Everett has left–I think."

K looked at this cool, aristocratic figure in his fine suit.

"Miss Everett has left–you think," K said.

"I heard her. We all heard her," Mr. Selkirk laughed.

"Whisky, Mr. Selkirk?" K asked.

"Yes, please."

"Ice?"

"Er–no, thanks. Just water, please. Thank you."

"What can you tell me about Mr. Gray?"

"A lot. What do you want to know?"

K looked at this aristocratic figure.

"A lot."

"Well, I didn't like him. I can tell you that. He was my sister's husband. But I didn't like Michael at all. I never liked him.

"Michael married my sister twenty-five years ago. He wasn't a rich man then–just out of the army. We– the family–took him into the firm. My father, James Selkirk, liked him. He worked hard. He became a Director of Selkirk Industries. Selkirk Industries is the family firm. Michael was a hard worker, but he married into money."

"You never liked him. Why?"

"A number of reasons. He often argued with Elizabeth, and I didn't like that at all. He liked women, and he spent a lot of money on them. But he spent money like water. I didn't like that. It's *our* money, the family's. He changed his will. My sister told me about it. He wanted to leave $200,000 to that silly girl, Angela Everett."

"His secretary."

"Yes—his secretary."

"Why did you come to Longacres, Mr. Selkirk?"

"He and I had a talk before dinner."

"I wanted to speak to Michael. He and I had a talk before dinner."

"Tell me about it."

cool *(adj.)* 冷淡的

aristocratic *(adj.)* 傲慢的、貴族氣習的

look up （抬頭）向上看

figure *(n.)* 人影、人形、人物

suit *(n.)* 西裝、一套衣服

at all 全然、不管怎樣；例句：
I don't like him at all. 我一點也不喜歡他。

He married into money. 他娶了有錢人。

spend *(v.)* 花費（過去式及過去分詞：spent）

silly *(adj.)* 愚笨的

$200,000　二十萬美金

You're going to leave $200,000 to your secretary, Elizabeth says. It isn't true?

Maybe it is.

But why?

She's good to me. It's my money and I can spend it.

It isn't your money. It's the family's.

I work hard -

Yes, but $200,000

It's family money.

Family money? It's my money. Without me Selkirk Industries will die.

That's not true. You can't spend money like that on women...

...Selkirk Industries could do without you. You should leave the firm!

Leave the firm! Ha! Ha!

Well, you can't leave $200,000 to that woman. I'll stop you.

Just try!

Cool face

冷漠的臉

CD ＊26

"Well, he's dead now, so that's good for Selkirk Industries."

"Yes, it's very good."

"And you're glad?"

"Yes. He's dead and I'm glad. The family firm is very important to me. Of course, I'm sorry for my sister. She really loved him. But it's good for the family."

"Did Mr. Gray leave $200,000 to Miss Everett?"

"I don't know. I haven't seen the will. He talked about it."

"Maybe Miss Everett is a rich woman now."

"Maybe she is."

"You're very cool, Mr. Selkirk."

"Cool?"

"Yes. He's dead and you're glad. Maybe he left $200,000 to his secretary. But you don't *look* angry. You really hated Mr. Gray, didn't you? Behind that cool face, you hated him?"

"True, but I didn't murder him."

"Behind that cool face, you hated him?"

"Mr. Gray died at 9:25. Where were *you* at the time?"

"Hasn't my sister told you? I was in the living room. She spoke to me about Everett. Then we heard Nancy–Mrs. Baker. We ran outside. We ran to the study door. Colonel Stevens and I broke down the door. We saw the body on the floor–there. Elizabeth called the police."

"Did you touch the body?"

"No. Michael was dead. We all saw that, and we didn't touch the body. We just waited for the police."

"And the police sent *me*."

"Yes, the police sent you."

"Yes, the police sent you."

"Thank you, Mr. Selkirk."

"Can we all go to bed now?"

"No, I'm sorry. It's late, but I have to speak to all of you. But first I have to speak to Mrs. Baker."

"I'll send her to you."

"Thank you, Mr. Selkirk."

behind *(prep.)* 在⋯後面

touch *(v.)* 碰觸、觸摸

Nancy Baker's story

南西·貝克的說辭

CD * 27

Nancy Baker's story:

"Whisky, Mrs. Baker?"
"Oh, yes, please. A large one."
"You like whisky, Mrs. Baker?"
"Er... well... I..."
"You often drink Mr. Gray's whisky...?"
"I... well... I..."
"Ice?"
"No, no, thank you. Well, yes, please."
K took the ice-tray out of the freezer. She took a piece of ice out of it and put it in the whisky.

"Look at this tray, Mrs. Baker."

"What about it, ma'am? I filled it this morning."

"Well, Mr. Gray died here—in front of the refrigerator. He had a glass of whisky in his hand. He wanted some ice, so he went to the refrigerator. He didn't get any ice."

"How do you know?"

"Look at this tray, Mrs. Baker."

"You and Miss Everett had ice in your whisky. That's two pieces. Mr. Gray didn't have any. That's strange, isn't it?"

"Yes, ma'am, it's very strange."

"How long have you been with the family?"

"Forty years."

"That's a long time."

"Yes, ma'am. Mrs. Gray was a little girl then—eight

"I love my Mrs. Gray."

years old, Andrew Selkirk was a baby. I worked for Mr. and Mrs. Selkirk. They're dead now."

"You like the family?"

"Yes. I love them all. I love my Mrs. Gray."

"And Mr. Gray? Did you love him?"

"Yes, ma'am. I loved him, too. They got married twenty-five years ago. I remember it well. I have worked for them since then. Mr. Gray was a good man. A kind man."

"He and Mrs. Gray often argued."

"Yes, ma'am. But he loved her deeply, and she loved him."

"But he liked pretty girls."

"He was a man."

"And Miss Everett? What about her?"

"Oh, I don't like *her*. I was always afraid of her."

"Afraid?"

"Yes, ma'am. She wasn't like the other girls. Mr. Gray *listened* to her. Maybe they'll run away and leave Mrs. Gray, I thought, and I didn't like that."

"You were afraid of it."

"Yes."

"Why?"

"Well...I clean this study every day, and..."

"And you always read Mr. Gray's letters?"

"I...er...yes, ma'am."

"Tell me about it."

"I'll try to remember."

"And you always read Mr. Gray's letters?"

a piece of 一塊

get married 結婚（過去式 got married）

since then 自那時候起

clean *(v.)* 打掃

A letter　一封信

It was last week when I was cleaning the study.

This desk! Oh! What's this? Mm. A letter. Her writing. I have to read it.

"Darling Mick—" The little...!

Darling Mick, I love you my darling Mick. I want to be with you. Can't we be together always. Can't we? You can leave ...at woman and we can ...e together. We can have ...h good times when ... in the ...

Suddenly the door opened and Mr. Gray came in.

What are you doing, Nancy?

Er...er...just cleaning the study, Sir.

I put the letter in my pocket.

I left the study and took it with me.

I read it in my room, then I put it back on Mr. Gray's desk...

...I was afraid.

Loyal housekeeper

忠心的管家

CD＊29

"Now they can't run away together. Are you glad, Mrs. Baker?"

"No, ma'am."

"No?"

"No, because Mr. Gray is dead. I didn't want Mr. Gray to run away with Miss Everett. But I didn't want him to die. I served him for twenty-five years."

"You're very loyal to this family, Mrs. Baker."

"Yes, ma'am. That's the word, 'loyal'. I don't know why. You see, I don't have a family. This *is* my family. Now I want to be with Mrs. Gray. Always. I want to help her. Miss Everett is a wicked woman. Mr. Gray is dead. She has taken Mr. Gray from us. She's really wicked, ma'am."

"Tell me about tonight, Mrs. Baker."

"Well, dinner was at 8:00. I served dinner, then I made some coffee for Colonel Stevens and some coffee for Mr. Gray. I always take–er–took–coffee to Mr. Gray after dinner. Mrs. Gray and Mr. Selkirk were in

"She's really wicked, ma'am."

the living room. They didn't want any coffee. I took the coffee to Colonel Stevens in the library. Then I went to the study with Mr. Gray's coffee. I knocked at the door, and he didn't answer. I tried to open the door, but it was locked — you know the story."

"Yes. You shouted, and three of the others came. Miss Everett didn't come."

"No, ma'am. She was in the garden — she says."

"She was in the garden, Mrs. Baker. Then Colonel Stevens and Mr. Selkirk broke down the door. And you saw Mr. Gray. He was there, just behind you, on the floor, dead!"

Mrs. Baker looked behind her and jumped. "Yes, ma'am. Just there!" She put her head between her hands and cried.

"You can go now, Mrs. Baker. Thank you."

Mrs. Baker looked behind her and jumped.

 serve *(v.)* 服務、服侍

loyal *(adj.)* 忠誠的、忠心的

wicked *(adj.)* 邪惡的

serve dinner 端出晚餐

took *(v.)* 這句話應該用「現在式」，但因女佣的語文程度有限，所以她說不準英文的時態。

jump *(v.)* 突然跳起

Your choice

你選擇誰？

C D ∗ 30

Who did it? Make your choice:

1.Mrs. Gray murdered her husband because:

a) she was jealous of Angela Everett. ☐

b) she hated him. ☐

c) her brother wanted it. ☐

2.Colonel Stevens murdered Mr. Gray because:

a) he was afraid of him. ☐

b) he didn't want to pay back the $100,000. ☐

c) he gambled. ☐

3. Angela Everett murdered Mr. Gray because:

a) she was jealous of Mrs. Gray. ☐

b) she wanted $200,000. ☐

c) she hated him. ☐

4. Andrew Selkirk murdered Mr. Gray because:

a) he didn't like him. ☐

b) he wanted to save his firm. ☐

c) he wanted to save his sister. ☐

5. Nancy Baker murdered Mr. Gray because:

a) she always read his letters. ☐

b) she drank a lot. ☐

c) she didn't want him to run away with Angela Everett. ☐

Who do you choose? X was

a) Mrs. Gray ☐

b) Colonel Stevens ☐

c) Angela Everett ☐

d) Andrew Selkirk ☐

e) Nancy Baker ☐

Answer: 1a, 2b, 3b, 4b, 5c

K's notes
K的筆記

C D ＊31

K's notes:

All these people have motives for the murder.

Mrs. Gray
Motive：Jealousy
Notes：Mrs. Gray really loved her husband, and he loved her. But he liked women, and Mrs. Gray was very jealous. She was jealous of all Mr. Gray's secretaries, but she was very jealous of Angela Everett. She wanted to punish her husband, so she murdered him.

Colonel Stevens
Motive：Money
Notes：Mr. Gray really wanted his money back and Colonel Stevens didn't want to pay it. He didn't want to sell his house. He gambled and lost the money in a silly way. He was afraid, so he murdered Mr. Gray.

Angela Everett
Motive：Money
Notes：She didn't love Mr. Gray, and he didn't love her. She only wanted his money. Did Mr. Gray leave money to her in his new will? Yes, Angela thought. She wanted $200,000, so she murdered Mr. Gray.

Andrew Selkirk

Motive：Loyalty to his family and to his firm, Selkirk Industries.

Notes：He's a cold man. He really didn't like Mr. Gray. Mr. Gray spent money like water, and he was worried about this. He wanted to save the firm, so he murdered Mr. Gray.

Nancy Baker

Motive：Loyalty to Mrs. Gray

Notes：She has served the Selkirks and the Grays for forty years. She really loves Mrs. Gray, and she loved Mr. Gray, but she hated Angela Everett. This question worried her: Is Mr. Gray going to run away with Everett? She wanted to stop this and to punish Mr. Gray, so she murdered him.

note *(n.)* 筆記

motive *(n.)* 動機

jealousy *(n.)* 嫉妒

punish *(v.)* 懲罰

loyalty *(n.)* 忠誠、忠心

worry *(v.)* 使憂慮、使煩惱

1：30

凌晨一點半

CD＊32

1：30, In the study:

"It's very late. I know and I'm sorry. I'm sorry for all this trouble. You're all tired. Please sit down. Mrs. Baker has brought us some coffee. That's very kind, Mrs. Baker. Thank you. It's late, and we all want to go

" I know the answer to this question."

to bed, but I have to speak to you. Of course, I spoke to you alone, one by one. There are three questions, and I have to answer them.

1.Who murdered Mr. Gray? One of you murdered him. You are sitting there. You are looking at me, and there is murder in your heart. Maybe I know your name, maybe I don't. I can't tell you yet.

2.Why did X murder Mr. Gray? You all have motives. Maybe you were jealous, maybe you wanted money, maybe you were loyal. I can't answer this question yet.

3.How did X murder Mr. Gray? Don't tell me. I can save you the trouble. I know the answer to this question now. I can tell you."

tired *(adj.)* 疲勞的

one by one 一個接一個地

save you the trouble 省掉你們的麻煩

Between 9:00 and 9:25
9:00至9:25之間

CD＊33

What happened between 9:00 and 9:25?

"Mr. Gray's death was strange. He was alone in the room, and the door and window were locked *from the inside*. X didn't come into the room and didn't leave the room at the time of the murder. X prepared the murder carefully. How did X prepare the murder? I know the answer—I think. You all know Mr. Gray's habits very well. Mr. Gray always went to his study after dinner. Sometimes his secretary went with him, but she didn't go with him tonight. Mr. Gray always had a drink and worked late. Mrs. Baker always brought him some coffee after dinner. What happened between 9:00 and 9:25? That's the question. I won't answer it yet. I want to say one thing. How tall was Mr. Gray? He was five feet ten inches tall. Now look at the refrigerator. How high is the freezer from the floor? It is four feet high. This is important. The freezer is in line with Mr. Gray's heart. What happened?"

Try to answer K's question–

Don't turn the page yet!

"The freezer is in line with Mr. Gray's heart."

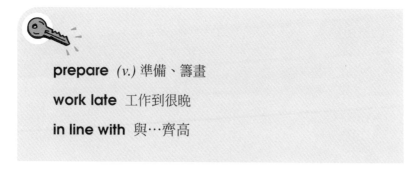

prepare *(v.)* 準備、籌畫

work late 工作到很晚

in line with 與…齊高

The icicle
冰柱

C D * 34

"Mr. Gray went into his study at 9:00. He locked the door and the window. Then at 9:02 he sat down at his desk and wrote. Then from 9:15 until 9:20 he used the dictaphone. At 9:20 he went to the liquor cabinet. He wanted some whisky. He poured some whisky into a glass and then water. He drank some. Then he wanted some ice. He opened the refrigerator. Then he opened the freezer. He pulled the ice-tray with his left hand and then what happened? He triggered a mechanism in line with his heart. This mechanism shot an icicle into Mr. Gray's heart. Mr. Gray turned and fell to the floor. He was dead. The glass fell out of his right hand. The icicle was in his heart, so there was blood and water on his shirt and blood and water on the carpet. There wasn't a murder weapon–there wasn't a gun or a knife. The sharp weapon was an icicle. It disappeared–and there was only water!

"The mechanism is still in the wall behind the freezer. You can't trigger it now. One of you put it

there. One of you came into this room before Mr. Gray and put it there. Who was it?" K asked. "I want to know."

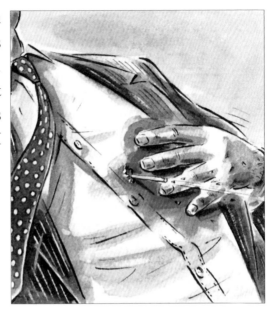

"This mechanism shot an icicle into Mr. Gray's heart."

pour *(v.)* 傾倒（水、酒）

trigger *(v.)* 觸發、觸動

mechanism *(n.)* 機關、機械裝置

icicle *(n.)* 冰柱

disappear *(v.)* 消失、不見

Everyone has a motive.

每個人都有動機

C D ＊35

"Was it you, Mrs. Gray?" K asked. "You were jealous of Mr. Gray's secretaries. You hate Angela Everett, and you wanted to punish your husband."

"No, no. I didn't do it. I loved him. I loved him."

"Was it you, Colonel Stevens? He gave you a lot of money. You gambled it on horses and lost it. He wanted it back."

"Of course not. He was my friend."

"And you, Miss Everett? He changed his will, and maybe he left you $200,000–a lot of money and you wanted it."

"I did it. You think that, don't you, policewoman? Well, I did it!"

"And you, Mr. Selkirk, always so cool, always so aristocratic? You were worried about the $200,000. You wanted to save the firm. Mr. Gray spent money on women, and you didn't like it."

Mr. Selkirk didn't answer.

"And you, Mrs. Baker? You read his letters. You

wanted to punish him."

"Oh, I didn't, really, I didn't. I didn't do it."

"Between 9:02 and 9:25 Mr. Gray wrote at his desk. What did he write? That's the question. He wrote a letter to Andrew Selkirk. I have it here. I'll read some of it to you. 'Dear Andrew, You're worried about money, I know. I changed my will two weeks ago, but I didn't leave any money to Angela. She thinks so, but I didn't. She's a silly girl and I'm tired of her. Maybe I need a new secretary...'"

"Oh!" Angela cried. "The pig! The pig!" She spat the word 'pig'.

tired of 厭倦的、厭煩的

spit (v.) 吐痰、吐口水、（像吐痰一樣）吐出（過去式及過去分詞：spat）

She cried.

她哭了！

CD＊36

"And at 9:15 he used his dictaphone. What did he dictate? Listen to his voice... 'Angela, darling. You're a nice girl and you've been good to me, but it can't go on. I am dictating this to you because I don't want to write a letter. I want to speak to you. I want to say goodbye to you. You're a young woman, and your life is in front of you. Goodbye, my darling. I only...'"

"Why? Why?" Angela screamed. "The pig! I hate him. I hate all of you! I hate you! I hate you!"

"You took him from me!" Mrs. Gray cried.

"Quiet!" Miss Everett shouted. "You can have him. He's dead! You and your family! You Grays and Selkirks. All so aristocratic! With your fine houses and your fine cars and your money! You can only think of money. He never loved me and I knew it. An old man of fifty-five! Pah! And I didn't love him. Yes, I wanted his money, but I couldn't have it. Of course, I didn't murder him. One of you did that. Thanks. You saved me the trouble. He's dead and I'm glad."

She ran out of the room.

Miss Everett put her face in her hands and ran out of the room. There were tears in her eyes.

Colonel Stevens got up. "No, don't follow her, Colonel Stevens," K said. "She won't leave. She can't leave. My people are all around the house."

"She called Mr. Gray a pig!" Mrs. Baker cried. "Did you hear? That woman called Mr. Gray a pig!"

pah *(interj.)* 哼！呸！（表示輕蔑、厭惡）

put her face in her hands 她以手掩面

There were tears in her eyes. 她眼裡噙滿淚水。

Goodnight

晚安

C D * 37

Goodnight:

K looked at her watch. It was 2:25. "We all have to go to bed," she said. "We're all tired." Then she spoke to Mrs. Gray. "It's very late, Mrs. Gray," K said, "and I can't leave this house. You all have to stay in the house, too. You can't leave, so don't try. There are police all around it. Where can I sleep, Mrs. Gray?" K asked. "I don't want to stay in this room."

"There's a room upstairs," Mrs. Gray said. "You can sleep there."

"Thank you, Mrs. Gray. Goodnight to you all," K said.

"Goodnight, Detective Kirby," they all said.

They all left the study and went to their bedrooms upstairs.

They went to their bedrooms upstairs.

 go to bed 上床睡覺、就寢

stay *(v.)* 逗留、待在（某處）

A figure in the dark

黑暗中的人影

CD＊38

A figure in the dark:

It was three o'clock in the morning. It was very dark, and the house was very quiet. K went downstairs quietly and went back to the study. She sat in Mr. Gray's chair and waited... 3:15... 3:30... 3:45... 4:00... 4:15... 4:30... K was very tired. She only wanted to sleep... to sleep... to sleep.

Suddenly she looked up! She heard a noise. It was the study door. The door opened very quietly. K saw a figure in the dark. It was the outline of a man! K could see very well in the dark. She watched and listened.

The figure went to the refrigerator. He pulled the refrigerator quietly from the wall. Then he pulled a small box out of the wall.

The mechanism!

He's come for the mechanism! K thought. She got up and went quietly to the figure. The man looked at the box and didn't hear K.

"Don't move!" K whispered. "Don't move, or..."

"Aaah!" the man cried. He tried to run out of the room.

Don't turn the page yet!

Who is the man in the dark? Make your choice!

Colonel Stevens

Andrew Selkirk

noise *(n.)* 噪音

get up *(n.)* 起身、站起來（過去式：got up）

whisper *(v.)* 低聲說、悄悄地說

A karate chop
一記空手道

C D＊39

K jumped on the man and held his arms. She knew her judo. A quick move, and the man was on the floor. Then a sharp karate chop! She hit the man hard in the neck!

"Aargh!" the man cried. Suddenly K turned on the light and looked down at the floor.

"Colonel Stevens!" she cried.

"Colonel Stevens!" she cried.

"Yes, it's me. Ooh! Please don't hit me again. You're a pretty little thing, but you know your judo... and that karate chop...Ooh!" Colonel Stevens touched his neck lightly.

"You came for the mechanism," K said. "I waited for you. I've been here since three o'clock. I was sleepy five minutes ago, but I'm not sleepy now!"

The mechanism was on the floor. Colonel Stevens took it in his right hand. "I didn't think..." he said. "I didn't think..." and his voice died away.

held his arms 抓住他的手臂

know *(v.)* 精通、擅長（過去式及過去分詞：knew, known）

judo *(n.)* 柔道

karate *(n.)* 空手道

chop *(n.)* 劈

sleepy *(adj.)* 想睡的、睏的

die away 逐漸消失

How?

行凶手法

CD＊40

The answer to K's first question: How...?

"Just a minute, Detective Kirby," Colonel Stevens said suddenly. "Look! I'm not the murderer. You don't think that, do you?"

"Why are you here?" K asked.

"I wanted to see this mechanism. I'm an engineer, remember? I tried to sleep, but I couldn't. Look at this mechanism! You see? It was behind the refrigerator. The box went into the wall, and this piece went into the back of the freezer. This string went on the ice-tray. Michael pulled the ice-tray, and this triggered the mechanism. It was in line with his heart. Look inside the box. See? It's a powerful bow. Very small, of course. And it shoots icicles! Michael opened the freezer, pulled the tray and WHAM! − an icicle through the heart! Then it turned to water and disappeared. The murder weapon just disappeared! Very clever!"

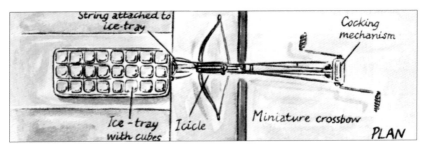

The mechanism

"Michael made this bow," Colonel Stevens said. "It's small but powerful. The murderer put an icicle in the freezer just before nine o'clock. Michael pulled the ice-tray. It was stuck in the freezer. Stuck with ice to the bottom of the freezer. So he pulled it hard. The icicle went into the string on the bow. The string went back and WHAM! The icicle went like an arrow. Very clever!"

"Mr. Gray made this bow?" K asked.

"Yes. He often made things like this in the army. It was his hobby." Suddenly Colonel Stevens stopped. He spoke slowly. "Michael made this bow, and it killed him. Who put it behind the refrigerator? Not me. Really, Detective Kirby, I didn't!"

"You didn't. I know." K said.

"Then who...?"

"I'll answer that question *now*!" K whispered. "Sh!" She walked to the door very quietly. Then she suddenly opened the door.

"Aaaah!"

There's a person outside the door. Who is it? Make your choice:

Mrs. Gray

Miss Everett

Andrew Selkirk

Nancy Baker

string *(n.)* 繩線

powerful *(adj.)* 有威力的

bow *(n.)* 弓

stick *(v.)* 陷住、卡住（過去式及過去分詞：stuck）

bottom *(n.)* 底部

arrow *(n.)* 箭

hobby *(n.)* 嗜好

attach *(v.)* 附著、繫上

cube *(n.)* 方塊、冰塊

cock *(v.)* 扳上扳機、扣發

miniature *(adj.)* 小型的

crossbow *(n.)* 十字弓、弩

Who?

凶手是誰？

CD＊41

The answer to K's second question: Who... ?

"Nancy!" K cried sharply.

"Oh!" Mrs. Baker cried.

"Nancy!" K said sharply. "Nancy! What are you doing?"

Mrs. Baker didn't answer.

"You're listening, aren't you, Nancy?"

"Yes, ma'am." Mrs. Baker said.

K pulled Nancy into the room. "Now answer me. Why are you listening?"

"I want to know... I want to know...

"Oh!" Mrs. Baker cried.

about the murder."

"Yes. You want to know," K said sharply. "This bow was in the wall behind the refrigerator. You wanted to take it out. And why did you want to take it out?"

Mrs. Baker didn't answer.

"You can't answer? Then I'll tell you. You wanted to take it out because you put it there. You put it there before nine o'clock last night."

Mrs. Baker still didn't answer.

"Didn't you?" K shouted.

"Yes, ma'am." Mrs. Baker whispered.

The lights went on all over the house. First Angela Everett came downstairs, then Andrew Selkirk, then Mrs. Gray. They all went into the study.

"Oh, I'm so sleepy," Miss Everett said. "What's happening? What's all this noise?"

Andrew Selkirk looked at the bow and then at Mrs. Baker. But he didn't speak. Mrs. Gray looked at the bow and then at Mrs. Baker.

"That's Michael's," she said. "He made it. He often made things like that. It was his hobby." She went to Mrs. Baker and held her arms. "Now look at me, Nancy," she said quietly. "Look into my eyes." Mrs. Baker looked up slowly. "Look into my eyes," Mrs. Gray said sharply. Mrs. Baker looked into Mrs.

Gray's eyes. "Now tell me. You didn't do it. Tell me that, please. Nancy. You didn't kill my husband."

"But I did, ma'am," Mrs. Baker said. "I killed him, but..."

"Nancy!" Mrs. Gray screamed. "Oh, Nancy! How could you, Nancy? How could you?" Mrs. Gray asked. "You've served my family for forty years. Nancy. You came to this family forty years ago. I was

"Look into my eyes."

a child of eight. Andrew was a baby. You love us. We love you. You've served Michael for twenty-five years. You loved him, too. Nancy, you couldn't do this wicked thing. You couldn't! You couldn't! Why, Nancy, why?"

"Oh, Mrs. Gray," Nancy said with tears in her eyes. "Mr. Gray made this powerful bow. I took it and

"Oh, Mrs. Gray," Nancy said with tears in her eyes.

made a plan. I came into this study last night at 8:50. You didn't hear me. I put an icicle in the freezer. I made the icicle in the big refrigerator in the kitchen. I put the mechanism in the wall behind the freezer a week ago. I prepared the mechanism a month ago. Last night I put the icicle into place. Last night was the night. I worked carefully and didn't leave any finger-prints. I've prepared a long time for last night."

"Yes, but *why* did you do it?" Mrs. Gray said.

scream *(v.)* 尖叫、尖聲地說

Why?

動機為何？

CD *42

The answer to K's third question: Why...?

"I didn't want to kill Mr. Gray. He wasn't my victim. I loved him and I love you. He wasn't always kind to you, and you often argued. He went with other women. I wanted to kill that woman there! That wicked woman, Everett. That was my motive. She usually came to the study with Mr. Gray. I knew their habits. She usually poured some whisky in a glass for Mr. Gray. She usually put some ice in the whisky. I prepared this mechanism very carefully for her, but last night *she didn't come*. She was in the garden. I didn't know that at the time. I was in the kitchen. At 9:30 I brought the coffee, and Mr. Gray didn't open the door. Then I knew. He was dead! Dead! And that woman, that wicked woman wasn't! Oh, Mrs. Gray, what could I do? What could I do?" Tears ran down Mrs. Baker's face.

"I wanted to kill that woman there!"

A policewoman went to her and whispered softly, "Come to the station with us now, Mrs. Baker." She took Mrs. Baker out of the room.

"What could I do? What could I do?" Mrs. Baker said again and again.

Goodbye

再 會

C D ∗ 43

Goodbye:

It's early morning. The sun is just coming up in the cold blue sky. A pretty girl is sitting in a fast sports car. She looks happy. The fast sports car is just outside Longacres. Three figures are standing beside the car: Mrs. Gray, Andrew Selkirk and Colonel Stevens. They say goodbye. The pretty girl speaks to Colonel Stevens. "Where's Miss Everett?"

"She's already gone," the Colonel said. "I called you 'a pretty little thing'–and you are!" Colonel Stevens laughed.

"Thank you, Colonel. I'm not on duty now. I've changed my clothes. That's the end of my first case. I'm not 'K' now. I'm Kathy Kirby. The day's just starting. Goodbye!"

"Goodbye!" the Colonel called.

Brrrm! The sound of the powerful engine broke the quiet of the morning. Brrm! Brrm! The powerful sports car disappeared into the early morning sun.

I'm not on duty now.

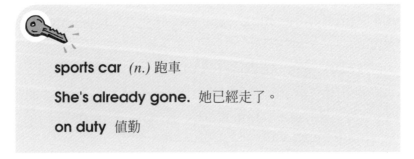

sports car *(n.)* 跑車

She's already gone. 她已經走了。

on duty 值勤

推理小說的定義

The definition of detective story is a fictional account of how a crime, usually a murder, is solved by an amateur or professional detective.

Detective story is a work of fiction about a puzzling crime, a number of clues, and a detective who eventually solves the mystery. In most detective stories, the crime is murder and the clues lead to or away from the solution.

The detective story, mystery, and suspense fiction originated in the mid-nineteenth century. Although its basic form has remained intact, the genre has branched into numerous subgenres: espionage, gothic, psychological suspense, police procedural, courtroom, whodunit, the conspicuously British drawing room mystery, and even to a certain degree the horror story. Each form has its practitioners, each its fans. Sometimes elements of these various genres are combined, themes are often intermingled, and mystery aficionados who usually tend to stick to what they like.

definition *(n.)* 定義

fictional *(adj.)* 虛構的

amateur *(adj.)* 業餘的

professional *(adj.)* 職業的

originate *(v.)* 發源、創始

intact *(adj.)* 完整無損的

subgenre *(n.)* 次分類

espionage *(n.)* 間諜活動

gothic novel 哥德式小說（強調神祕、淒涼、怪異）

whodunit *(n.)* 推理小說（或電影、戲劇；音同 who done it）

drawing room （接待賓客用的）大客廳、交誼廳

Each form has its practitioners, each its fans.
每一類型都有人寫，每一類型也各有它的讀者。

intermingled *(adj.)* 混合的

aficionado *(n.)* 熱愛者

▶ 測驗部分

聽力測驗

請先看一遍問題，接著聽該段CD一遍，然後開始作答。

最後再聽一遍CD，同時檢查答案及補充未作完的問題：

CD＊1

1. How old was the murder victim?

(a) fifty   (b) twenty-five   (c) fifty-five   (d) sixty-five
(e) forty-eight

CD＊3

2. How old is Elizabeth Gray, the victim's wife?

(a) fifty   (b) twenty-five   (c) fifty-five   (d) sixty-five
(e) forty-eight

CD＊3

3. How old is Angela Everett, the victim's secretary?

(a) fifty   (b) twenty-five   (c) fifty-five   (d) sixty-five
(e) forty-eight

CD＊4

4. At what time did Mrs. Baker take Mr. Gray some coffee on the night he died?

(a) 10:15 (b) 9:02 (c) 9:50 (d) 9:30 (e) 8:00

CD＊6

5. How many bedrooms are there at "Longacres"?

(a) four rooms (b) five rooms (c) eight rooms

(d) three rooms (e) six rooms

CD＊14

6. Who was in the garden when the murder happened?

(a) Elizabeth Gray (b) Colonel Stevens (c) Angela Everett (d) Andrew Selkirk (e) Nancy Baker

CD＊18

7. What did Mr. Gray do before he worked at Selkirk Industries? He was...

(a) in the army (b) teaching (c) jobless (d) at school

(e) a bartender

CD＊18

8. Colonel Stevens borrowed money from Mr. Gray. What did he do with it?

(a) bought a house (b) gave to his mother (c) deposited in the bank (d) gambled on horses (e) bought a car

CD＊27

9. How long has Nancy Baker worked for Mrs. Gray's family?

(a) seven years (b) twenty-five years (c) fifteen years
(d) forty years (e) fourteen years

CD＊28

10. How did Mrs. Baker find out that Angela Everett wanted to run away with Mr. Gray?

(a) She heard them talking about it. (b) Mrs. Gray told her. (c) She read Miss Everett's letter. (d) She saw them meeting secretly. (e) Mr. Gray told her.

CD＊34

11. What was the weapon for the murder?

(a) knife (b) icicle (c) gun (d) club (e) poison

CD＊40

12. Who made the bow which killed Mr. Gray?

(a) Elizabeth Gray (b) Colonel Stevens (c) Mr. Gray
(d) Andrew Selkirk (e) Nancy Baker

CD＊41

13. Who was the murderer?

(a) Elizabeth Gray (b) Colonel Stevens (c) Angela Everett (d) Andrew Selkirk (e) Nancy Baker

CD＊42

14. Who did the murderer really want to kill?

(a) Elizabeth Gray (b) Colonel Stevens (c) Angela Everett (d) Andrew Selkirk (e) Mr. Gray

解答：

1. c 2. e 3. b 4. d 5. c 6. c 7. a 8. d 9. d
10. c 11. b 12. c 13. e 14. c

▶ 測驗部分

閱讀與寫作測驗

【本書內容簡介】：

Mr. Michael Gray is dead. He was the victim of a murder and he was very rich. Who murdered him? Kathy Kirby-or 'K' as she is called-is a detective and she wants to find the murderer. Was it Mr. Michael Gray's wife, Elizabeth Gray? Or was it his secretary? Or his housekeeper? Or his wife's brother? Or his friend?

英文寫作測驗：

1. 請先閱讀以上【本書內容簡介】，文中包括四個單字及基本定義：

detective: *(n.)* a police officer who investigates crimes

housekeeper: *(n.)* a servant who is employed to perform domestic task in a household

secretary: *(n.)* an assistant who handles correspondence and clerical work for a boss or an organization

murderer:*(n.)* a criminal who commits homicide,

especially the unlawful premeditated killing of another human being

請參考這些字的定義，以簡短文字敘述這些人所扮演的角色。

2. 請用英文寫一篇約 150－200 字的新聞報導，敘述一九八二年十一月十七日發生在豪宅「長畝」（Longacres）裡的凶殺案，到底是誰謀殺了麥可・葛瑞先生 （Mr. Michael Gray）？而美麗的女警探 K 究竟如何破了此案？

3. 本書裡的許多圖片底下都有說明文字（caption），而這些文字幾乎都是從內文裡挑出來的短句。請挑選十張不同的圖片，用你自己的話來寫圖片解說。

▶ 中文翻譯

被害人

CD*1

劇中人物:

這是一則謀殺故事。

這名男子是被害人。
他的名字叫麥可‧葛瑞。
他今年五十五歲,非常有錢。
他是謝爾柯克工業公司的董事。

女警探

CD*2

看這名女子。
她年輕又漂亮,而且非常聰明。
她是一個警探。

她的名字叫凱西‧柯比。

人們叫她 K。

她想要找出一些重要問題的答案。

這是她的第一件案子。

你能幫助她嗎？

K，我們這位聰明的警探，提出三個重要的問題：

X 謀殺了被害人麥可‧葛瑞，那麼，

1. X 用什麼方法謀殺了葛瑞先生？

2. 誰是 X？

3. X 為什麼要謀殺葛瑞先生？

行凶手法？凶手是誰？動機爲何？

誰是X？

CD＊3

行凶手法？凶手是誰？動機為何？

誰是 X？

謀殺案發生了，當時房子裡還有其他五個人，其中一個是 X。他到底是誰？

伊麗莎白・葛瑞，
她是麥可・葛瑞的妻子，
今年四十八歲。

威廉・史蒂文斯上校，
他是葛瑞先生的朋友，
今年五十歲。
他以前在軍中服務，
但現在已經離開軍中了。

安琪拉・艾佛瑞小姐，
她是葛瑞先生的祕書，
已經做了一年了。
她今年二十五歲。

安德魯・謝爾柯克先生，
他是葛瑞太太的弟弟，
今年四十歲。
他也是謝爾柯克工業
公司的董事。

南西‧貝克太太，
她是葛瑞家的管家。
她在葛瑞太太家已做了
四十年，今年六十歲。

發生了什麼事？

CD＊4

發生了什麼事？

日期：一九八二年十一月十七日
現在時刻：十點十五分
地點：新英格蘭區的一座大鄉村宅邸

今天晚上八點，葛瑞先生和其他四人一塊用餐。然後他走進書房，那時是九點鐘。他從屋裡把門鎖上，也把窗子關上，並從裡面鎖上。

九點半，管家貝克太太端咖啡到他房間。她敲門，葛瑞先生沒有應聲，因此她再敲一次，並大聲喊叫。他還是沒有回答，她就叫其他三人過來。他們也敲門並大聲喊叫，但葛瑞先生還是沒有開門。他們破門而入，看到葛瑞先生趴在地板上，人已斷了氣。

葛瑞太太打電話報警，時間是九點四十分。警方在九點五十分抵達，K 跟他們一起抵達。

警方查到了什麼？

ＣＤ＊5

現在是十點十五分，K 正在書房裡。

葛瑞先生的屍體現在已經不在這裡，警方拍下書房及屍體的照片，然後把屍體移到警察局。法醫已經驗過屍，警方已經查出三個重要問題的答案：

1. 葛瑞先生不是死於中毒。九點二十分他喝了些威士忌，但威士忌裡沒有毒藥，葛瑞先生的血液裡也沒有毒藥的跡象。

2. X 用一把尖銳的凶器刺進葛瑞先生的心臟。

3. 葛瑞先生死於九點二十五分。

一位警察從警察局打電話給 K。「我們知道三件事，」警察說，「第一件是：並非中毒。第二件是：是一把尖銳的凶器──刺入心臟。第三件是：葛瑞先生死於九點二十五分。」

葛瑞先生的房子

CD＊6

這棟房子：

看這張葛瑞先生家的照片。這是一棟大房子，名字叫「長畝」，樓上共有八個臥房。樓下有門廳和廚房，還有四個大房間──餐廳、客廳、書房和藏書室。

這是樓下房間的平面圖，請仔細看。今天晚上八點鐘，葛瑞先生和其他四人一塊兒在餐廳裡用餐。接著，他在九點鐘進入書房。

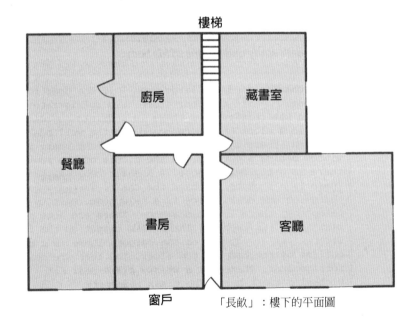

「長畝」：樓下的平面圖

書房與謀殺

CD＊7

書房與謀殺：

這宗謀殺案發生在葛瑞先生的書房。這是警方拍下的書房照片，請仔細看，並描述書房內的情景，然後再讀 K 的報告。

葛瑞先生的書房和他屍體的輪廓圖

（K 的報告）

葛瑞先生的書房很大，有扇門作爲入口。門的旁邊是冰箱，冰箱的旁邊是酒櫃，酒櫃上面有鐘。酒櫃附近的牆上有一幅圖畫。右邊窗簾後面是窗戶。房間中央有張大書桌，桌後有椅子，椅子背後是書櫃。書桌上擺了一些物品，有電話，電話旁是口述錄音機，有一些紙張放在口述錄音機旁。地板上鋪著地毯。

葛瑞先生的屍體趴在地毯上。地板上有警方畫的屍體輪廓圖，雙腳離冰箱很近。葛瑞先生的右手附近有一個威士忌酒杯，杯裡是空的。

線　索

ＣＤ＊８

線索：

現在仔細看這些線索，把他們一一寫出來，然後再讀 K 的報告。

K 發現了這些事情：

葛瑞先生的襯衫上有血跡和水漬。Ｘ刺進葛瑞先生的心臟，襯衫上有個洞。

葛瑞先生右手邊的地板上有空的威士忌酒杯，杯裡有少許威士忌和水漬。

地毯上有血跡和水漬。

門從裡面鎖上。

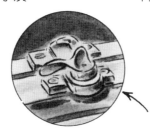

窗戶從裡面鎖上。

K 沒有發現這些事情：

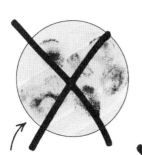

沒有其他指紋，
只有葛瑞先生的。

沒有任何凶器，
沒有刀或槍。

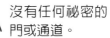

沒有任何祕密的
門或通道。

鎖上的房間

CD＊9

（K的報告）

葛瑞先生的屍體在冰箱前面，雙腳靠近冰箱，臉朝下趴在地毯上。

威士忌酒杯是空的，我聞過了。命案發生的時候，酒杯就在葛瑞先生的右手上，他的襯衫上——在心臟的位置——有血跡和水漬。X用一把尖銳的凶器刺死葛瑞先生。地毯上有血跡和水漬。X用一把尖銳的凶器刺殺葛瑞先生，因此葛瑞先生的襯衫上沾有血跡，地毯上也有血跡。但是，為什麼葛瑞先生的襯衫及地毯上也都有水漬呢？

葛瑞先生從屋裡把門鎖上，把窗戶也鎖上。書桌上、冰箱上和威士忌酒杯上有指紋，但這些都只是葛瑞先生的指紋。房間裡沒有任何祕密通道，也沒有刀或槍。葛瑞先生的口述錄音機還開著。

K正在為她的報告寫筆記。

K的第一個理論

ＣＤ＊10

事情是這樣發生的嗎？Ｋ的第一個理論：

9:00　葛瑞先生進入書房，從裡面把門鎖上。

9:02　他關上窗戶，從裡面鎖上。

9:05　他坐在書桌前寫東西，然後使用口述錄音機。

9:20　他走向酒櫃，倒了一杯威士忌酒小酌。

9:22　他向冰箱走去，想要一些冰塊。

9:25　Ｘ進入書房，用一把尖銳的凶器刺殺葛瑞先生，
　　　然後離去。

9:30　貝克太太敲門，呼喚其他三人過來。

9:35　他們破門而入。

9:40　葛瑞太太打電話報警。

9:50　警方和Ｋ趕到現場。

這個理論正確嗎？那麼Ｘ用什麼方法進入書房，他或她又是如何出去的？窗戶和門都從裡面鎖上，沒有任何祕密的門或通道。為什麼葛瑞先生的襯衫上和地毯上都有水漬呢？

其他的理論

CD＊11

其他的理論：

K 的第一個理論不太周全。請你想一想其他理論，然後與 K 的理論作個比較。

K 的第二個理論

這是自殺。不對。為什麼？因為威士忌酒裡沒有任何毒藥，而葛瑞先生的血液裡也沒有中毒的跡象。葛瑞先生有用刀子嗎？沒有。為什麼？因為房間裡沒有刀，所以不是自殺。

K 的第三個理論

X 原先就在房裡，他或她用刀殺了葛瑞先生，然後離去。是 X 把刀（或尖銳的凶器）帶走了。不對。為什麼？門是從裡面鎖上，窗戶也是從裡面鎖上。

K 的第四個理論

X 從鑰匙孔開門進來。不對。為什麼？鑰匙還插在鑰匙孔裡。

你有想到其他理論嗎？

你有把你的理論拿來和 K 的作比較嗎？

比較的結果呢？

麥可・葛瑞的習慣

ＣＤ＊12

麥可・葛瑞的習慣

K 的報告：

今天晚上，葛瑞先生在七點鐘回到家。他和他的祕書安琪拉・艾佛瑞一起回來。葛瑞先生總是在這個時間回到家，但他的祕書不一定跟著他回來。

史蒂文斯上校和安德魯・謝爾柯克兩人都已經在「長畝」，他們是下午五點來的。他們和葛瑞太太小酌一會，貝克太太把酒端到藏書室裡。

七點時，葛瑞先生進入房間。他洗澡更衣，準備用晚餐。他總是在這個時候洗澡和換衣服。然後他進入藏書室，和太太、史蒂文斯上校、安德魯・謝爾柯克及安琪拉・艾佛瑞一起喝一杯。葛瑞先生總是在餐前喝一杯酒。

晚餐在八點鐘開始。葛瑞先生總是在八點用晚餐。在餐廳裡，眾人圍桌而坐，邊吃邊聊天。

貝克太太答問

ＣＤ＊13

貝克太太答問：

　　Ｋ坐在書房裡葛瑞先生的椅子上，和貝克太太談話。

　　「所以他們邊吃邊聊，貝克太太？」Ｋ問她。

　　「是的，小姐。」貝克太太說。

　　「他們有彼此談笑嗎，貝克太太？」

　　「哦，是的，小姐。他們都是好朋友。」

　　「好朋友，貝克太太？」

　　「是的──是這樣，嗯──葛瑞先生和葛瑞太太，是這樣──他們……」

　　「他們吵架，貝克太太？」

　　「是的，小姐，但不是在吃晚餐時。晚餐後，葛瑞先生和葛瑞太太走進藏書室，只有他們兩個人。他們吵了起來，我聽見了。那時我是在廚房裡。他們互相對吼，我們都聽見了。」

　　「然後呢？」

　　「然後葛瑞先生走進他的書房。」

　　「那時幾點了？」

　　「九點。」

繼續追問

ＣＤ＊14

「葛瑞先生總是在九點進入他的書房嗎？」

「是的，小姐。他在書房工作到凌晨一點或兩點，有時候他的祕書也跟他一起到書房裡去。」貝克太太說。

「有時候？今晚她有一塊兒進去嗎？」

「沒有，小姐。九點半時，我端咖啡去給葛瑞先生，每次我總是在九點半端一杯咖啡給他喝。我敲書房的門，他沒有回答。我敲了一遍又一遍，大聲喊叫，他還是沒有回答，所以我就叫葛瑞太太、史蒂文斯上校和謝爾柯克先生過來。」

「那艾佛瑞小姐人呢？」

「她沒有過來，小姐。當時她在花園裡。史蒂文斯上校和謝爾柯克先生破門而入，我們發現他——葛瑞先生——我們發現他倒在地板上——死了！哦！」貝克太太哭了，她非常傷心。

「謝謝妳，貝克太太。」K輕聲說。

伊麗莎白・葛瑞的說辭

ＣＤ＊15

伊麗莎白・葛瑞的說辭：

貝克太太離開書房，Ｋ繼續寫她的報告。然後有人敲門，很輕很輕地敲門。

「進來。」Ｋ輕聲地說。門開了。

「妳想見我。」葛瑞太太說。

「是的，葛瑞太太，請進來坐下。要不要喝一杯？」

「不要，謝謝。」

「妳好嗎？」Ｋ輕聲地問。

「妳怎麼可以這樣問？麥克走了，他死了，死了！這不是真的，是不是，柯比警探？這不是真的。」

「噓！」Ｋ說，「告訴我關於他的事。」

「麥克？他是個好丈夫。我們二十五年前結婚，那是很久以前的事了，不是嗎？那時候他剛從軍中退伍，他愛我，我也愛他。我們沒有子女，麥克一直覺得很遺憾，可是他對我始終是個好丈夫。」

「自始至終？」

「是的，自始至終！」葛瑞太太抬高了聲音：「是這樣——有……」

「是的？」K 輕聲地問。

「其他的女人，所有這些祕書！」葛瑞太太大聲說。「麥克一直喜歡年輕的祕書——她們也喜歡他，為了他的錢！看現在這個新祕書，這個……這個……她叫什麼名字？這個安琪拉‧艾佛瑞。這個小……！」葛瑞太太的聲音沉默下來，可是她的臉漲紅，眼裡充滿怒氣。

「哦，」她說，「我恨麥克的祕書，她們個個年輕，個個漂亮，她們把他從我這裡搶走。可是，我真正恨的是現在這個祕書，這個安琪拉‧艾佛瑞。她每天都到我家裡，和麥克一起來。『對不起，葛瑞太太，』她柔聲細氣地說，『我必須把葛瑞先生從妳這裡帶走，我們有事要忙。』麥克愛我，我知道！我知道！但他也喜歡別的女人。

「妳想見我。」葛瑞太太說。

我愛他，但我也恨他。

他有錢，所以女人也喜歡他。是的，我愛他，但有時候我恨
他，我恨他！也許他現在就在這房間裡，也許他可以聽見我
說話。我愛他，但我也恨他，他心裡明白。」

「今晚發生了什麼事？」Ｋ問。

「我說給妳聽。」葛瑞太太說。

晚餐後

麥克，我可以跟你談一談嗎 ──到藏書室裡？

是的，麗絲。

什麼事，麗絲？

是關於……這個……這個祕書。

安琪拉？ 是的

她是個邪惡的女人，麥克。我很清楚，她要你的錢。

那不是真的，麗絲。

是的！我很清楚。

她是個好祕書，麗絲。我工作時少不了祕書。

我不喜歡她，麥克，她很邪惡。

唔，我喜歡她，她是我的祕書。

求求你，麥克，我不想吵架。

我沒有吵架，是妳要吵的。

請聽我的話，麥克。

我不想聽，妳永遠都是這樣，妳在嫉妒。

妳在嫉妒。

我沒有……不要大聲吼。

我沒有大聲吼。

我要去書房了，我有事要忙。

求求你，麥克，請聽我說……我很抱歉。

＊麗絲（Liz）：伊麗莎白（Elizabeth）的暱稱
＊麥克（Mike）：麥可（Michael）的暱稱

叫警察

CD＊17

「所以，葛瑞先生在九點鐘進入他的書房，那時妳在做什麼？」K問。

「我去客廳，我想跟我弟弟安德魯談談。我們坐下來談話，我告訴他關於麥克和那個女人艾佛瑞的事，安德魯全都知道了。」

「葛瑞先生人在書房裡，妳聽得見他嗎？」

「聽不見。直到九點半，南西大叫，安德魯和我才趕到書房。但門鎖著，安德魯和史蒂文斯上校破門而入，然後我看到麥克整個人趴在地板上，死了！我打電話報警。」

「艾佛瑞小姐在哪兒？」K問。

「在花園裡。晚餐後她經常直接到書房裡去。」

「但今晚沒有？」

「沒有，今晚沒有，她在花園裡。為什麼麥克會死？那不是自殺，也許她知道內情，也許她可以告訴妳。那樣的女人對這個家沒什麼好處。我可以離開了嗎？」葛瑞太太猛然問。

「當然，」K說，「謝謝妳，葛瑞太太。」

史蒂文斯上校的說辭

ＣＤ＊18

史蒂文斯上校的說辭：

此刻是十點四十五分，有人敲書房的門。

「我可以進來嗎？」有個聲音問道，是男人的聲音。

「是的。」Ｋ說。

門開了，進來的是史蒂文斯上校。「今晚妳要見我們每一位，柯比警探？」

「是的。」Ｋ說。「想喝一杯嗎，史蒂文斯上校？」

「是的，麻煩妳。」

「威士忌？」

「是的，麻煩妳了，我需要喝一杯！」

「冰塊？」

「冰塊？嗯，嗯，謝謝妳，不用了。我不要任何冰塊，只要水就可以了，麻煩妳，謝謝。」

「他是你的朋友？」Ｋ問。

「是的，而且是非常要好的朋友。」上校說，他雙手捧著頭，「死了！麥可·葛瑞死了！我真不敢相信。」

「的確令人悲傷，」Ｋ說，「卻是事實。」

「告訴我關於他的事。」Ｋ說。

「死了！麥可‧葛瑞死了！我真不敢相信。」

　　「我們一起在軍中服務，那是二十五年前的事了。後來麥可離開軍中，娶伊麗莎白為妻，進入謝爾柯克工業公司，那是葛瑞太太的家族企業，她是謝爾柯克家的人。我五年前離開軍中，現在已經不算是軍人，但大家還是叫我『上校』。我需要工作，所以找上老友麥可，他幫了我的忙。」

　　「幫你？如何幫法？」K問。

　　「哦──嗯──唔，錢，妳知道的。」

　　「我不知道。」K說。

　　「他給我錢。」

　　「給你？」

　　「借我。」

　　「他借你多少錢？」

　　「十萬美金。」

　　「嗯，那你如何使用那些錢？」

「我拿去做生意。」

「你做什麼生意，史蒂文斯上校？」

「啊，那不能算是真正的生意……馬……妳知道的。」

「你拿去賭馬。」Ｋ的語氣尖銳。

「是的，我賭輸了，」上校說，「麥可曉得這件事，他對我非常生氣。他說：『我借你的這筆錢，現在你非還我不可。』我說：『不行，我沒有錢！』他說：『那你得賣掉你的房子！』我並不想賣房子，我們為這件事吵了起來。」

「他現在死了，」Ｋ說，「你真的難過嗎？」

「難過？我當然難過。我們為錢爭吵，但我們還是朋友，好朋友。軍中同袍永遠都是好朋友。」

「你在軍中是做什麼的，上校？」

「我在工兵部隊，麥可也是在工兵部隊。」

「你是工程師？」

「我幹過工程師。」

「而現在你拿別人的錢去賭博。」Ｋ尖銳地說。

「我賭輸了。」

「你和葛瑞先生為錢吵架，告訴我當時的情形。」

賭輸了錢

你輸掉了！我現在就要那筆錢，你現在非還我不可！

求求你，麥可，你不會損失那筆錢的。

喂，威廉，我借給你十萬美金，我的錢呢？

我現在沒有錢。

我現在就要，你必須賣房子還我。

我不能那樣做！我現在還不能還給你。

但是，麥可，求求你，想想以前的日子，我們是老朋友了，記得嗎？

你非還我不可！

我不管那些，我只要我的錢。

你賭掉了十萬美金。

沒錯，我賭輸了，但是——

我的錢！

別叫那麼大聲，老頭。

不要叫我『老頭』，你要快點拿出那筆錢來！

漂亮的小姑娘

ＣＤ＊20

「告訴我今晚的情形。」

「今晚？晚餐後我和安德魯一起到客廳，麥可和伊麗莎白到藏書室去。他們倆吵了起來，我們從客廳都可以聽見他們。麥可和伊麗莎白經常吵架。麥可──妳知道的──他喜歡拈花惹草，而安琪拉，嗯，她是個漂亮的小姑娘。」上校笑著說，「就像妳，柯比警探，漂亮的小姑娘。」

「謝謝你，上校。」Ｋ微笑道。「晚餐後你在做什麼？」

「唔，麥可去他的書房，伊麗莎白到客廳，而我到藏書室裡，坐下來閱讀。」

「一個人？」

「是的，一個人。九點半時，管家貝克太太端咖啡給我，然後她端去給麥可。他的門鎖著，她大聲叫喊，我跑去書房。接下來發生的事，妳都已經知道了。」

「是的，但我不知道所有發生的事──尚未知道！」Ｋ辭鋒銳利。「你現在可以離開了，上校，請幫我叫艾佛瑞小姐過來。」

安琪拉・艾佛瑞的說辭

ＣＤ＊21

安琪拉・艾佛瑞的說辭：

「我不喜歡這個房間，」艾佛瑞小姐說，「米克死在這裡，就在兩小時之前──米克死在這裡。妳為什麼要用這個房間？」

「我有我的理由。」Ｋ說。「坐下，艾佛瑞小姐，要不要喝一杯？」

「是的，請給我一大杯威士忌和許多冰塊。」

Ｋ走過去，打開冰箱，然後打開冷凍庫，拿出製冰格。Ｋ放了一些冰塊在艾佛瑞小姐的酒裡，然後把製冰格放回冷凍庫。Ｋ檢查一下冷凍庫，然後朝艾佛瑞小姐看。

「妳幹嘛看我？」艾佛瑞小姐猛然問。

「史蒂文斯上校說妳是『漂亮的小姑娘』，妳是嗎？」Ｋ抬高了聲音。

「那妳呢？」艾佛瑞小姐問，她也抬高了聲音。

「是我在問妳問題。」Ｋ回答。「這是妳的酒。」

「謝謝。」

「他愛妳。」

「他當然愛我，她沒告訴妳嗎？」

「她？」

「那個女人，他老婆。她不愛他，她總是跟他吵，她總跟我的米克吵來吵去。」

「米克？」

「是的，他是我的『米克』，她的『麥克』，其他人的『麥可』。我的米克愛我。她總是大聲對他吼，跟他吵架，所以他總是來找我。她給他恨，我給他愛。」

「妳真的愛他嗎？」

「當然，我深深愛他，她也知道。我恨她，我恨那個女人。」艾佛瑞小姐大聲說，「她恨我的米克，而我恨她。她謀殺了他，我知道，一定是她。」

「葛瑞先生五十五歲，而妳才二十五。」

「妳在說些什麼？」艾佛瑞小姐語氣尖銳地說。「難道妳不認識任何五十五歲的好男人嗎？米克人很好，真的很好。」

「而且有錢。」Ｋ挑明地說，「他留了一大筆錢給妳，在他的遺囑裡。」

「真的嗎？妳怎麼知道？」

「我在問妳問題，妳要回答。」Ｋ說。「妳知道錢的事。」

「是的。」艾佛瑞小姐回答。

「他留給妳多少錢？」

「我不知道。」

「妳很清楚，告訴我。」Ｋ抬高了聲音。

「米克在兩個星期前更改遺囑，當然他留了大筆錢給她。她並不需要錢，她已經很富有。可是他也留了二十萬美金給我，他告訴過我。」

「葛瑞先生現在已經去世，那對妳而言是一件很好的事。」

「對我是好事？妳在說些什麼？我愛他，難道妳不明白嗎？」

「是的，但也許妳現在已經發財了，也許妳已經有了二十萬美金。」

「嫉妒嗎？」艾佛瑞小姐尖刻地問 K。「聽著，女警察，我愛錢，那是事實，但我愛米克，妳聽見了嗎？我愛米克。為什麼警方要派一個女警探來？」

「妳去問他們。」K 說。

「聽著，女警察，我愛錢。」

「妳長得漂亮，」艾佛瑞小姐說，「我的米克喜歡漂亮的女人。他老婆以前也是個漂亮的女人，現在已經不是了。」

「我一定要跟她說。」Ｋ說。

「好啊，去跟她說，拜託妳去跟她說！」

「妳經常在晚餐後跟葛瑞先生一起到書房裡去。」

「是的，我們一起工作。我們通常在九點鐘到書房裡去，我通常陪米克喝一杯，然後開始工作。管家通常在九點半端咖啡給我們。我工作到十一點，然後回家。」

「但是，妳今晚沒有去葛瑞先生的書房。」

「沒有，我沒去，這事很奇怪。」

「奇怪？」

「是的，米克不讓我去，他想一個人獨處。」

「告訴我當時的情形。」

註：這段情節提到Ｋ放了一些冰塊（some ice）在艾佛瑞小姐的威士忌酒裡，但在ＣＤ＊２７，Ｋ卻又說只給了艾佛瑞小姐一塊冰塊，顯然作者有些矛盾。

回家途中

我們今晚要工作嗎？米克。

工作？不用了，安琪拉。

今晚我想一個人工作。

米克……

什麼事？

你要弄你的遺囑嗎？

也許吧。

我的小米克愛他的安琪拉。

那還用說。

小米克不會再更改他的遺囑吧？

我不想談我的遺囑。

我的米克愛他的安琪拉，不愛那個女人。

安琪拉！我早就告訴過妳，不要把伊麗莎白說成那樣！

米克！小心點！

SCREEECH

安琪拉！有時候我對妳非常火大！

修改遺囑

ＣＤ＊23

「那妳今晚在哪兒──當謀殺案發生的時候？」

「在花園裡。」

「花園的哪個地方？」

「就在米克書房的外面。」

「為什麼？」

「我想走一走。夜很涼，但星空晴朗，我需要呼吸空氣。米克在他的書房裡，我想跟他在一起，我一個人，我不想留在屋子裡。」

「妳擔心。」Ｋ說。

「擔心？為什麼？」

「也許葛瑞先生想再度更改他的遺囑，妳擔心這件事，妳不想要他更改，對不對？」

「妳錯了，我只是想跟他在一起，跟錢無關。」

「妳想要成為有錢的女人。」

「閉嘴！」艾佛瑞小姐大聲說，「我長得漂亮，所以妳恨我。妳喜歡她。哼，聽著，不是我幹的，明白嗎？我沒有殺他！」艾佛瑞小姐叫道，然後跑出了房間。

安德魯・謝爾柯克的說辭

ＣＤ＊24

安德魯・謝爾柯克的說辭：

「我可以進來嗎？」這個人的聲音冷漠而傲慢。

「可以，請把門關上。」Ｋ說著，抬起頭來。

「是我，安德魯・謝爾柯克。艾佛瑞小姐已經離開了──我想。」

Ｋ看著這個冷漠傲慢的男士，一身剪裁合身的高級西裝。「艾佛瑞小姐已經離開了──你想。」Ｋ說。

「我聽見了，我們全都聽到她大吼大叫。」謝爾柯克先生笑著說。

「來杯威士忌，謝爾柯克先生？」Ｋ問。

「是的，麻煩妳了。」

「要不要冰塊？」

「嗯──不用了，謝謝。只要水就好了，謝謝妳。」

「你可以告訴我多少關於葛瑞先生的事？」

「很多。妳想知道什麼？」

「很多。」

「噢，我不喜歡他，我老實告訴妳。他是我姊夫，可是我一點都不喜歡麥可。我從來都不喜歡他。

「麥可二十五年前娶了我姊姊，那時他沒有錢──他剛退伍。我們——我們家族——把他帶進公司。我父親詹姆斯·謝爾柯克喜歡他。他工作努力，成為謝爾柯克工業公司的董事。謝爾柯克公司是家族企業，麥可雖然是個努力的人，但他娶了有錢人家的女兒，才有今天。」

「你從來都不喜歡他，為什麼？」

「一堆理由。他經常和伊麗莎白吵架，這點我很不喜歡。他喜歡拈花惹草，在女人身上花了許多錢。他花錢如流水，這我不喜歡，那是我們的錢，我們家的錢。他更改遺囑，我姊姊跟我說了這件事，他想留二十萬美金給那個愚蠢的女孩安琪拉·艾佛瑞。」

「他的祕書。」

「是的——他的祕書。」

「你為什麼到長畝來，謝爾柯克先生？」

「我想和麥可談談，我們倆在晚餐前談了一陣。」

「告訴我你們談話的情形。」

「我們倆在晚餐前談了一陣。」

二十萬美金　　　ＣＤ＊25

伊麗莎白說，你要留二十萬美金給你的祕書。這是真的嗎？

但為什麼呢？

她對我很好，那是我的錢，我想花就花。

也許是吧。

那不是你的錢，那是家族的錢。

我辛苦工作——

沒錯，但是二十萬美金！

那是家族的錢。

家族的錢？那是我的錢。沒有我，謝爾柯克工業公司早就倒了。

那不是真的。你不能把錢花在女人身上。

謝爾柯克工業公司沒有你照樣營運，你應該離開公司！

離開公司！哈！哈！

哼，你不能留二十萬美金給那個女人，我要阻止你。

試試看！

冷漠的臉

ＣＤ＊26

「好啊，他現在死了，這對謝爾柯克工業公司是件好事。」

「是的，非常好。」

「你很高興？」

「是的，他死了，我很高興。這個家族企業對我非常重要。當然我為我姊姊感到難過，她真的愛他，不過這對整個家族是件好事。」

「葛瑞先生真的留給艾佛瑞小姐二十萬美金？」

「我不知道。我還沒看到遺囑，他有提過這事。」

「也許艾佛瑞小姐現在已經是富婆了。」

「也許她是的。」

「你很冷漠，謝爾柯克先生。」

「冷漠？」

「是的。他死了，你卻很高興。也許他留給他的祕書二十萬美金，但你好像不生氣。你真的很恨葛瑞先生，是不是？在你那張冷漠的臉孔背後，你其實很恨他？」

「說得對，但我沒有謀害他。」

「葛瑞先生死於九點二十五分，那時你在哪裡？」

「我姊姊沒有告訴妳嗎？我當時在客廳裡，她跟我提艾佛瑞的事，然後我們就聽到南西──貝克太太──大叫。我們跑出來，趕到書房門口。史蒂文斯上校和我破門而入，我們看到地板上的屍體──就在那兒。伊麗莎白打電話報警。」

「你有去碰屍體嗎？」

「沒有，麥可死了，我們都看到了。我們沒有去碰屍體，只是在那兒等警方來。」

「而警方派我來。」

「是的，警方派妳來。」

「謝謝你，謝爾柯克先生。」

「現在我們可以去睡覺了嗎？」

「不行，我很抱歉。時間很晚了，但我必須和你們每一位談話。首先，我要和貝克太太談談。」

「我幫妳叫她來。」

「謝謝你，謝爾柯克先生。」

南西‧貝克的說辭

ＣＤ＊27

南西‧貝克的說辭：

「要不要來一杯威士忌，貝克太太？」

「哦，好的，請給我一大杯。」

「妳喜歡威士忌，貝克太太？」

「唔……啊……我……」

「妳常喝葛瑞先生的威士忌？」

「我……啊……我……」

「冰塊？」

「不，不要，謝謝妳。啊，好吧，麻煩妳。」

K從冷凍庫拿出製冰格，從中取出一塊冰塊，放入威士忌裡。

「貝克太太，看看這個製冰格。」

「怎麼啦，小姐？我今天早上倒了水進去。」

「嗯，葛瑞先生在這裡死去──在冰箱前面。他手上拿著一杯威士忌，想加點冰塊，所以他走向冰箱，可是他沒有拿走任何冰塊。」

「妳怎麼知道？」

「妳和艾佛瑞小姐都在威士忌裡加了冰塊，總共是兩塊，所以葛瑞先生一塊都沒有拿。那有點奇怪，不是嗎？」

「是的，小姐，非常奇怪。」

「妳在這個家做多久了？」

「四十年。」

「那是漫長的時間。」

「是的，小姐。那時候葛瑞太太還是個小女孩──才八歲，安德魯‧謝爾柯克只是個嬰兒。我當時為謝爾柯克夫婦工作，他們現在已經過世了。」

「妳喜歡這家人？」

「是的，我愛他們每一個人，我愛我的葛瑞太太。」

「那葛瑞先生呢？妳愛他嗎？」

「是的，小姐，我也愛他。他們在二十五年前結婚，我記得很清楚，從那時起我就服侍他們。葛瑞先生是個好人，一個親切和藹的人。」

「他和葛瑞太太經常吵架。」

「是的，小姐。但他深深愛她，而她也愛他。」

「可是他喜歡漂亮的女孩。」

「他是男人啊！」

「那艾佛瑞小姐呢？妳對她有何看法？」

「哦，我不喜歡她，我一直怕她。」

「怕？」

「是的，小姐。她不像其他的女孩，葛瑞先生對她言聽計從。我以為，也許他們會私奔，拋棄葛瑞太太。我不喜歡那樣。」

「妳擔心這事會發生。」

「是的。」

「為什麼？」

「嗯……我每天來打掃書房，而……」

「而妳總是偷看葛瑞先生的信？」

「我……唔……是的，小姐。」

「告訴我詳細情形。」

「我想想看。」

一封信

CD＊28

那是上星期的事，我正在打掃書房。

書桌……哦！這是什麼？嗯，一封信，她的筆跡，我一定要看。

「米克，達令──」這個小……！

突然間，門開了，葛瑞先生走進來。

妳在做什麼，南西？

唔……唔……只是在打掃書房，先生。

我把信放在我的口袋裡。

我離開書房，把信帶走。

我拿到我房間裡看，然後把它放回葛瑞先生的書桌上……

……我很擔心。

忠心的管家

ＣＤ＊29

「現在他們不能一起私奔了，妳高興嗎，貝克太太？」

「沒有，小姐。」

「沒有？」

「沒有，因為葛瑞先生死了。我不希望葛瑞先生和艾佛瑞小姐私奔，可是我也不希望他死，我在葛瑞家做了二十五年呢！」

「妳對這個家非常忠誠，貝克太太。」

「是的，小姐，就是這個字：『忠誠』。我不知道為什麼。妳知道，我沒有自己的家，這裡就是我的家。現在我只想陪著葛瑞太太，永遠陪著她。我想幫助她。艾佛瑞小姐是個邪惡的女人，葛瑞先生死了，她把葛瑞先生從我們這裡帶走了，她真的很邪惡，小姐。」

「告訴我今晚的情形，貝克太太。」

「嗯，晚餐在八點鐘開飯。我服侍他們用餐，然後我幫史蒂文斯上校和葛瑞先生煮咖啡。我總是在晚餐後端咖啡給葛瑞先生。葛瑞太太和謝爾柯克先生那時在客廳裡，他們不想喝咖啡。我端咖啡到藏書室給史蒂文斯上校，然後又端到書房給葛瑞先生。我敲門，他沒有回答。我試著打開門，可是門鎖著──接下來發生的事，妳都知道了。」

「是的，妳大喊，其他三人趕到，艾佛瑞小姐沒有過來。」

「沒有，小姐。她在花園裡——據她說。」

「她在花園裡，貝克太太。接著，史蒂文斯上校和謝爾柯克先生破門而入，妳看到葛瑞先生，他在那兒，就趴在妳背後的地板上，死了！」

貝克太太往後看，跳了起來。「是的，小姐，就在那裡！」她手抱著頭，哭了。

「妳可以離開了，貝克太太，謝謝妳。」

你選擇誰？

ＣＤ＊30

是誰幹的？由你作選擇：

1. 葛瑞太太謀殺了她的丈夫，因為

a）她嫉妒安琪拉·艾佛瑞

b）她恨他

c）她的弟弟指使她

2. 史蒂文斯上校謀殺了
   葛瑞先生，因為
a）他怕他
b）他不想還十萬美金
c）他賭博

3. 安琪拉‧艾佛瑞謀殺
   了葛瑞先生，因為
a）她嫉妒葛瑞太太
b）她想要二十萬美金
c）她恨他

4. 安德魯‧謝爾柯克謀
   殺了葛瑞先生，因為
a）他不喜歡他
b）他想拯救他的公司
c）他想救他的姊姊

5. 南西・貝克謀殺了葛瑞先生，因為

a）她總是偷看他的信

b）她偷喝太多酒

c）她不希望他和安琪拉・艾佛瑞私奔

你選擇誰？X 是

a）葛瑞太太

b）史蒂文斯上校

c）安琪拉・艾佛瑞

d）安德魯・謝爾柯克

e）南西・貝克

解答：1a, 2b, 3b, 4b, 5c

K的筆記

CD＊31

K的筆記：

這些人都有謀殺的動機。

葛瑞太太

動機：嫉妒

筆記：葛瑞太太眞的很愛她的丈夫，而他也愛她。但他喜歡拈花惹草，葛瑞太太非常嫉妒。她嫉妒葛瑞先生的每一個祕書，但她特別嫉妒安琪拉・艾佛瑞。她想懲罰她的丈夫，所以謀殺了他。

史蒂文斯上校

動機：金錢

筆記：葛瑞先生很想把錢要回來，而史蒂文斯上校並不想還錢。他不想賣掉自己的房子，他愚蠢地把錢拿去賭博，輸個精光。他很擔心，所以謀殺了葛瑞先生。

安琪拉・艾佛瑞

動機：金錢

筆記：她不愛葛瑞先生，他也不愛她。她只要他的錢。
　　　葛瑞先生有沒有在新遺囑裡留給她一筆錢呢？有
　　　的，安琪拉如此想。她想要得到二十萬美金，所
　　　以謀殺了葛瑞先生。

安德魯・謝爾柯克

動機：忠於他的家族及謝爾柯克工業公司

筆記：他是個冷漠的人，他著實不喜歡葛瑞先生。葛瑞
　　　先生花錢如流水，而他對這點很擔心。他想要拯
　　　救公司，所以謀殺了葛瑞先生。

南西・貝克

動機：忠於葛瑞太太

筆記：她在謝爾柯克家及葛瑞家總共服務了四十年。她
　　　真的愛葛瑞太太，也愛葛瑞先生，但她恨安琪
　　　拉・艾佛瑞。這個問題困擾著她：葛瑞先生會和
　　　艾佛瑞一起私奔嗎？她想阻止此事和懲罰葛瑞先
　　　生，所以謀殺了他。

凌晨一點半

ＣＤ＊32

凌晨一點半，在書房裡：

「我知道時間已經很晚了，很抱歉。我很抱歉麻煩了各位。你們都累了，請坐下。貝克太太幫我們端來了咖啡，妳真好，貝克太太，謝謝妳。時間已晚，我們都想睡了，可是我還有話跟你們說。當然，我已經和你們個別談過話。有三個問題，我必須作答。

1. 誰謀殺了葛瑞先生？你們其中一位謀殺了他，你坐在那兒，看著我，心裡有數。也許我知道你的名字，也許我不知道，現在我還不能告訴你。

2. Ｘ為什麼要謀殺葛瑞先生？你們每一位都有動機。也許你們是嫉妒，也許你們想要錢，也許你們是出於忠誠。現在我還不能回答這個問題。

3. Ｘ用什麼方法謀殺了葛瑞先生？不用告訴我，我可以省下你們的事。我現在已經知道這個問題的答案了，我可以告訴你們。」

9:00至9:25之間

ＣＤ＊33

在 9:00 至 9:25 之間發生了什麼事？

「葛瑞先生的死因相當離奇。他獨自在房間裡，門和窗戶都從裡面鎖上。謀殺發生之際，Ｘ 既沒有進來房間也沒有出去。Ｘ 縝密籌畫這椿謀殺案，他如何籌畫呢？我想——我知道答案。你們都很清楚葛瑞先生的作息，葛瑞先生總是在晚餐後進到他的書房。有時候他的祕書跟他一起進去，但她今晚沒有。葛瑞先生總是會喝上一杯，而且工作到很晚。貝克太太總是在晚餐後端咖啡給他。在九點至九點二十五分之間發生了什麼事？問題就在這裡，我還不想回答。我要說明一件事。葛瑞先生有多高？他是五呎十吋高。現在看這個冰箱，冷凍庫離地面有多高？有四呎高。這很重要，冷凍庫與葛瑞先生的心臟位置一樣高。發生了什麼事？」

試著回答 K 的問題——

還不要翻到下一頁！

9.00

9.00

9.02 – 9.15

9.15 – 9.20

9.20 –

9.25

冰柱　　　　　　　　　　CD＊34

　　「葛瑞先生在九點鐘進入他的書房，他鎖上門和窗戶。九點零二分，他在書桌前坐下，寫東西。接著，從九點十五分至九點二十分，他使用口述錄音機。九點二十分，他向酒櫃走去，想喝威士忌。他倒了些威士忌酒到玻璃杯裡，然後摻上水。他喝了一些，接著他想加冰塊。他打開冰箱，然後打開冷凍庫，用左手拉出製冰格，接著發生了什麼事？他觸動了與他心臟位置齊高的機關。這個機關射出一支冰柱刺入葛瑞先生的心臟。葛瑞先生轉身，倒在地板上，死了。玻璃杯從他的右手掉下去。冰柱刺入他的心臟，所以他的襯衫上有血跡和水漬，地毯上也有血跡和水漬。現場沒有凶器──沒有槍或刀。殺人的利器是一根冰柱，它消失無蹤──只剩下一些水跡！

　　「這個機關仍然在冷凍庫後面的牆壁上，但現在已不能再啓動了。你們其中一位把它裝設在那兒，你們其中一位在葛瑞先生進到書房之前先進來，把它裝在那兒。是誰？」K問道，「我想知道。」

每個人都有動機

CD＊35

　　「是妳嗎，葛瑞太太？」K問，「妳嫉妒葛瑞先生的祕書們，妳恨安琪拉・艾佛瑞，還有妳想懲罰妳的丈夫。」

「沒有，沒有，我沒有殺他！我愛他，我愛他！」

「是你嗎，史蒂文斯上校？他給你許多錢，你拿去賭馬，賭輸了，他卻想把錢要回去。」

「當然沒有，他是我的朋友。」

「至於妳，安琪拉・艾佛瑞，他更改他的遺囑，也許他留給妳二十萬美金──一大筆錢，妳想要拿到手。」

「是我殺的，妳認為是我，對不對，女警察？好吧，是我殺的！」

「至於你，謝爾柯克先生，總是如此冷漠，如此傲慢，你擔心那二十萬美金，你想要拯救公司，而葛瑞先生把錢花在女人身上，你看不過去。」

謝爾柯克先生沒有回答。

「至於妳，貝克太太，妳偷看他的信，妳想懲罰他。」

「哦，我沒有，真的，我沒有，我沒有殺他。」

「在九點零二分至九點二十五分之間，葛瑞先生在他的書桌上寫東西，他寫什麼呢？那就是問題的所在。他寫了一封信給安德魯・謝爾柯克。信就在我手上，我唸其中幾段給你們聽。『親愛的安德魯，你在擔心錢的事，我知道。我在兩星期前更改遺囑，可是我沒有留半毛錢給安琪拉。她以為有，其實不然。她是個愚蠢的女孩，我已經厭倦了她。也許我要再找一個新祕書……』」

「哦！」安琪拉高喊著，「豬！這隻豬！」她口沫橫飛地吐出「豬」這個字。

她哭了！

ＣＤ＊36

「九點十五分，他使用口述錄音機。他口述什麼呢？聽他的這段錄音……『安琪拉，達令，妳是個好女孩，對我一直很好，但我們不能再繼續下去。我口述這段話給妳，因為我不想寫信。我想跟妳說，我要跟妳分手。妳是個年輕的女子，眼前有長遠的人生。再見，我的達令，我只……』」

「為什麼？為什麼？」安琪拉尖叫著，「這隻豬！我恨他，我恨你們每一個人！我恨你們！我恨你們！」

「妳把他從我這裡搶走了！」葛瑞太太大聲說。

「閉嘴！」艾佛瑞小姐大叫著，「給妳好了，他已經死了！妳和妳的家族！你們葛瑞家和謝爾柯克家，個個都是如此傲慢！你們有豪宅、高級轎車和鈔票！你們滿腦子只有錢。他從來沒有愛過我，我知道。一個五十五歲的糟老頭！呸！我也不愛他。是的，我要他的錢，可是我拿不到手。當然，我沒有謀殺他，是你們其中一個做的好事。謝啦，你們幫我省了麻煩。他死了，我樂得開心。」

艾佛瑞小姐眼裡噙滿淚水，她以手掩面衝出了房間。

史蒂文斯上校站起身來。「不必了，不必去追她，史蒂文斯上校。」Ｋ說，「她不會離去，她也不能離去，整棟房子周圍都是我的人。」

「她叫葛瑞先生豬！」貝克太太叫道，「你們聽見了嗎？那個女人叫葛瑞先生豬！」

晚 安

ＣＤ＊37

晚安：

Ｋ看一下表，兩點二十五分。「我們都得去睡了，」她說，「我們都累了。」然後她轉向葛瑞太太，「時間已晚，葛瑞太太，」Ｋ說，「我不能離開這棟房子，你們也都要留在屋子裡。你們不能離開，所以不必試了，周圍都是警察。我可以睡哪裡，葛瑞太太？」Ｋ問道，「我不想留在這個房間裡。」

「樓上有個房間，」葛瑞太太說，「妳可以睡那裡。」

「謝謝妳，葛瑞太太。晚安，各位。」Ｋ說。

「晚安，柯比警探。」眾人齊聲說。

他們全都離開書房，到樓上各自的臥房裡。

黑暗中的人影

ＣＤ＊38

黑暗中的人影：

凌晨三點鐘，周遭一片漆黑，房子裡寂靜無聲。Ｋ悄悄下樓，回到書房裡。她坐在葛瑞先生的椅子上等待……三點十五分……三點半……三點四十五分……四點鐘……四點十五分……四點半……Ｋ筋疲力竭，她只想睡覺……睡覺……睡覺。

忽然間，她抬起頭來！她聽到一個聲響，是書房的門！門悄悄打開了，Ｋ看到黑暗中出現一個人影。那是一個男子的身影！在黑暗中，Ｋ也看得一清二楚。她盯著，聆聽動靜。

這個人影走向冰箱，他悄悄地把冰箱推離牆壁，然後從牆上拉出一個小盒子。

那個機關！

他是來取機關的！Ｋ心想。她站起身來，悄然移向人影。男子正在打量盒子，沒有聽到Ｋ走近。

「別動！」Ｋ輕聲說，「別動，否則……」

「啊哎呀！」男子叫出聲來，他想跑出屋外。

還不要翻到下一頁！

黑暗中的男子是誰？作出你的選擇！

史蒂文斯上校

安德魯・謝爾柯克

一記空手道

ＣＤ＊39

　　Ｋ一躍而上，抓住他的手臂。她擅長柔道，一個快動作，男子已摔倒在地。接著，又是一記敏捷的空手道！劈在男子的脖子上！

　　「啊啊哎！」男子尖叫。一瞬間，Ｋ開亮了燈，往地板上看。

　　「史蒂文斯上校！」她叫道。

　　「是的，是我。哦！求求妳不要再打我了。妳是個漂亮的小姑娘，可是妳會柔道……那記空手道……哦！」史蒂文

184

斯上校輕輕撫摸自己的脖子。

「你為機關而來，」K說，「我正在等你，從三點等到現在。五分鐘前我睡意正濃，但我現在睡意全消。」

機關掉在地上，史蒂文斯上校用右手撿起來。「我不認為……」他說，「我不認為……」他的聲音越來越弱。

行凶手法

ＣＤ＊40

K的第一個問題：行凶手法？答案是……

「等等，柯比警探，」史蒂文斯上校猛然說，「妳瞧，我並不是凶手，妳不這樣認為吧？」

「為什麼你要來這裡？」K問。

「我想看看這個機關。我是個工程師，記得嗎？我想睡覺，卻睡不著。看看這機關，妳明白了嗎？它裝設在冰箱的後面，盒子釘在牆上，而這根冰從冷凍庫後面穿進來，用繩線套在製冰格上。當麥可拉出製冰格，就觸動了機關，它剛好和他的心臟位置齊高。看這個盒子的裡面，明白嗎？這是一支威力強大的弩弓，體積很小，想當然爾，但它能射出冰柱！麥可打開冷凍庫，拉出製冰格，碰！一支冰柱穿過心臟！接著，冰柱融成水，消失無影。凶器就這樣不見了！非常高明！」

「麥可製作了這支弩弓，」史蒂文斯上校說，「它體積雖小，但威力強大。凶手就在九點前把一支冰柱放進冷凍庫，麥可拉出製冰格時，製冰格卡在冷凍庫裡，和冷凍庫底部的冰卡在一起，所以他用力拉。冰柱移到弩弓的弦線上，當弓弦反彈，碰！冰柱就像箭一樣射出，非常高明！」

「葛瑞先生製作這把弓？」K問。

「是的，他在軍中經常製作這些玩意兒，那是他的嗜好。」史蒂文斯上校突然停下來，他緩緩地說：「麥可製作這把弓，它卻殺了他。誰把弓放在冰箱的後面？不是我，真的，柯比警探，我沒有！」

「你沒有，我知道。」K說。

「那到底是誰呢？」

「我現在就回答這個問題！」K壓低了聲音：「噓！」她悄悄走向門口，猛然打開門。

「啊啊呀！」

門外有個人，到底是誰？由你作選擇：

伊麗莎白・葛瑞

安琪拉・艾佛瑞

安德魯‧謝爾柯克　　　　　南西‧貝克

凶手是誰？

ＣＤ＊41

　　Ｋ的第二個問題：凶手是誰？答案是……

　　「南西！」Ｋ尖聲叫道。

　　「哦！」貝克太太大叫。

　　「南西！」Ｋ銳聲說道，「南西！妳在做什麼？」

　　貝克太太默不作聲。

　　「妳在偷聽，對不對，南西？」

　　「是的，小姐。」貝克太太說。

　　Ｋ把南西拉進房裡。「現在回答我，妳為什麼要偷聽？」

　　「我想知道……我想知道……關於謀殺的事。」

　　「是的，妳想知道。」Ｋ銳聲說道，「這把弓裝設在冰箱

的後面，妳想把它取下。為什麼妳想取下它？」

貝克太太沒有答話。

「妳無法回答？那我告訴妳。妳想取走它，因為那是妳裝設的。昨晚九點以前，妳把它裝在那裡。」

貝克太太依然沒有回答。

「是不是？」K 提高聲音。

「是的，小姐。」貝克太太低聲說。

整棟屋子的燈光全亮了。首先是安琪拉‧艾佛瑞跑下樓來，接著是安德魯‧謝爾柯克，然後是葛瑞太太。他們全都趕到書房裡。

「哦，我好睏，」艾佛瑞小姐說，「怎麼回事？為什麼這麼吵？」

安德魯‧謝爾柯克看一眼弩弓，然後看著貝克太太，但他沒有開口。葛瑞太太看一眼弩弓，然後看著貝克太太。

「那是麥可的東西，」她說，「他做的，他經常製作這些玩意兒，那是他的嗜好。」她走到貝克太太身邊，抓住她的手臂。「現在，看著我，南西。」她輕聲地說，「看著我的眼睛。」

貝克太太緩緩抬起頭來。「看著我的眼睛！」葛瑞太太抬高了聲音。貝克太太看著葛瑞太太的眼睛。「現在告訴我，妳沒有做這件事。求求妳，告訴我，南西，妳沒有殺了我的丈夫。」

「可是是我做的，太太。」貝克太太說，「我殺了他，但是……」

「南西！」葛瑞太太尖叫，「哦！南西！妳怎麼可以這樣，南西？妳怎麼可以？」葛瑞太太問：「妳在我家做了四十年，南西。妳四十年前就來到這個家，那時我是個八歲小孩，安德魯還是個嬰兒。妳愛我們，我們也愛妳。妳服侍麥可也有二十五年了，妳也愛他。南西，妳不可以做出如此邪惡的事。妳不可以！妳不可以！為什麼？南西，為什麼？」

「哦，葛瑞太太，」南西眼裡流著淚說，「葛瑞先生製作這把威力強大的弩弓，我拿到手，就開始籌畫。昨晚我在八點五十分進入書房，你們都沒有聽見。我把一支冰柱放進冷凍庫裡，冰柱是我在廚房的大冰箱裡做好的。一個星期前，我把機關裝設在冷凍庫後面的牆壁上。一個月前我準備好機關。昨晚我把冰柱放在位置上，昨晚就是我計畫實施之夜。我非常小心，沒有留下任何指紋。我籌畫許久就是為了昨晚。」

「是的，但妳為什麼要這樣做？」葛瑞太太說。

「看著我的眼睛。」

動機為何？

CD＊42

　　Ｋ的第三個問題：動機為何？答案是……

　　「我並不想殺葛瑞先生，他不是我的下手對象。我愛他，我也愛妳。他沒有一直善待妳，你們經常吵架，而他又招惹其他女人。我要殺的是那個女人！那個邪惡的女人艾佛瑞。那就是我的動機。她通常和葛瑞先生一起進入書房，我了解他們的作息。她通常幫葛瑞先生倒一些威士忌到玻璃杯裡，也通常在威士忌裡加冰塊。我這個機關就是專為她精心準備的，可是昨晚她沒有進來，她在花園裡。那時我並不知道，因為我在廚房裡忙著。九點半，我端咖啡過來，葛瑞先生沒有開門，我這才知道不好了！他死了！死了！而那個女人，那個邪惡的女人卻沒事！哦，葛瑞太太，我該怎麼辦？我該怎麼辦？」貝克太太淚流滿臉。

　　一名女警走過來，壓低了聲音對她說：「現在請妳跟我們到警察局去，貝克太太。」她把貝克太太帶出房間。

　　「我該怎麼辦？我該怎麼辦？」貝克太太一遍又一遍地說。

再 會

CD＊43

再會：

清晨時分，太陽剛從冷冷的藍天冒出來。一個漂亮的女郎坐在快速跑車上，她看起來很開心。跑車停在「長畝」的外面，三個人影站在車旁：葛瑞太太、安德魯・謝爾柯克和史蒂文斯上校。他們在向女郎道別。這個漂亮的女郎對史蒂文斯上校說：「艾佛瑞小姐呢？」

「她先走了，」上校說，「我叫妳『漂亮的小姑娘』──妳當之無愧！」史蒂文斯上校笑道。

「謝謝你，上校。我現在不當班，我已經換了便服。我的第一件案子已到此為止，我現在不是 K，我是凱西・柯比。今天剛展開序幕呢，再見！」

「再見！」上校大聲說。

噗噗噗！馬力十足的引擎聲音劃破寂靜的早晨。噗噗噗！噗噗噗！馬力十足的跑車消失在清晨的陽光中。

Studying系列 ⑲

成寒英語有聲書4 — 推理女神探

編　　著—成寒
主　　編—張敏敏
編　　輯—林文理
美術編輯—黃昶憲・林麗華
專案企劃—查美鳳

發 行 人—趙政岷
出 版 者—時報文化出版企業股份有限公司
108019台北市和平西路三段二四〇號一至七樓
發行專線—（〇二）二三〇六—六八四二
讀者服務專線—〇八〇〇—二三一—七〇五・（〇二）二三〇四—七一〇三
讀者服務傳眞—（〇二）二三〇四—六八五八
郵撥—一九三四四七二四時報文化出版公司
信箱—10899台北華江橋郵局第九十九信箱
時報悅讀網—http://www.readingtimes.com.tw
法律顧問—理律法律事務所　陳長文律師、李念祖律師
電子郵件信箱—popular@readingtimes.com.tw
印　　刷—勁達印刷有限公司
初版一刷—二〇〇四年二月二十三日
初版十九刷—二〇二三年五月二十九日
定　　價—新台幣二三〇元

版權所有　翻印必究（缺頁或破損的書，請寄回更換）

時報文化出版公司成立於一九七五年，
並於一九九九年股票上櫃公開發行，於二〇〇八年脫離中時集團非屬旺中，
以「尊重智慧與創意的文化事業」爲信念。

成寒英語有聲書. 4, 推理女神探 / 成寒編著. —
初版. — 臺北市：時報文化, 2004[民93]
　　面 ；　　公分. —（Studying系列 ; 19）

　　ISBN 978-957-13-4067-8（平裝附光碟片）

1. 英國語言 - 讀本

874.57　　　　　　　　　　93001784

ISBN 978-957-13-4067-8
Printed in Taiwan